ZOE'S ZODIAC

MARY JO STEPHENS

Illustrated by Leonard Shortall

1971

HOUGHTON MIFFLIN COMPANY BOSTON

For my father and mother

CONTENTS

●

AQUARIUS • 1

PISCES • 33

ARIES • 50

TAURUS • 60

GEMINI • 77

CANCER • 92

LEO • 117

VIRGO • 127

LIBRA • 141

SCORPIO • 167

SAGITTARIUS • 191

CAPRICORN • 209

AQUARIUS

●

January 21 – February 19

1

You won? Zoe, you actually won?" Ruthie squealed. "I don't believe it! Let me see."

Ruthie threw her notebook to the floor, snatched the evening paper from Zoe, and plopped down on the bottom stair.

"Don't tear it," Zoe said. "Daddy has fits if anything happens to his precious paper." She sat down slowly beside Ruthie and stared at her own name, in block letters an inch high, right in the middle of page eight.

"Ruthie, I never won anything in my life! Well, except a gym award last year, and everybody got one of those."

"I didn't," Ruthie corrected, cracking her gum. "I hit Elmer with a softball, remember? But he deserved it. Zoe, this is the craziest prize I ever heard of. Well, what's the matter? You don't look very happy."

"I'm not." Zoe spread the newspaper carefully on the hall rug before them. She pulled her single long braid over her shoulder and nibbled nervously on the curl at the end. "They'll never let me have this prize. I may as well forget it."

"Not let you have it? What are you talking about? ference to my father."
They *have* to! You won it!"

Zoe shook her head. "That's not going to make any dif-
"But that's no fair!"

"Since when are parents fair?"

"Oh. I see what you mean." Ruthie concentrated on blowing a large pink bubble. As she peeled the gum from her nose, she said, "Well, you'll just have to persuade him. There are ways, you know."

"That's what you think. You know Daddy better than that, Ruthie."

"You always talk like your father's the original mean-old-man-of-the-mountain, Zoe. Now, honestly, did he ever *do* anything to you? All I've ever seen him do is yell and wave his glasses."

"That's just it, Ruthie. I never know when he means what he says and when he doesn't."

Ruthie turned to face Zoe on the stair. "You don't understand men. All they want is to make people think they are the chief head leaders. As long as their children let them *act* like the boss and they can keep up their image, you can get whatever you want."

Zoe frowned and chewed on her braid. "Keep up their image?"

"Sure," said Ruthie. "All men do it. Your dad, too. You know your mother just lets him yell and says 'yes, dear,' and then she goes right ahead and does whatever she wants. And Bob and Marcia — "

"Bob is too sensible to ask for anything like this," Zoe said, pointing to the paper. "And Marcia's disgusting! She sits on his lap and messes up his hair and calls him a pussy cat — "

"And gets exactly what she wants." Ruthie nodded approvingly. "Marcia understands men. Of course, she's older."

"I'll never understand my father if I live to be a hundred."

"What's to understand?" Ruthie shrugged her shoulders. "I just explained him. I think your mother just has him around for a pet."

"Don't mention that word!"

"Sorry. But it brings us to the point. Now, let's get organized." Ruthie tried another bubble while she thought. "Can you get your mother on your side?"

"As long as the prize doesn't interrupt her schedule, she's no worry. It's Daddy."

"O.K., then. You just have to think of all the excuses he's going to come up with, and have an answer ready for them. Easy."

"Daddy doesn't give reasons or excuses. Just says no. Mother says he's a law unto himself."

"Oh, come on! He *has* to give some reasons — they'll get in his way, or you won't take care of them, or something. All you have to do is answer everything he says with logic."

Zoe chewed on her braid. "It might work."

Ruthie shrugged again. "Sure. And if logic fails, try tears. You can cry better than anybody I know. Do it now, Zoe. I love to see you cry!"

Zoe threw her braid back over her shoulder, where it hung to her waist, and stared wide-eyed at the front door in front of her. Through the glass top of the door she could see the snow-covered pine tree in the front yard. She sighed deeply and in a moment a small but genuine tear trickled down her left cheek.

Ruthie applauded. "How do you *do* that, Zoe? I'd love to be able to cry whenever I want to. It must be so handy!"

"Stare straight ahead. Don't blink. Now, think of something sad."

Ruthie's eyes bulged. "Like what?"

Zoe looked out at the snow again. "Think of all the frozen prisoners in Siberia."

Ruthie blinked and shook her head. "It's no use. All I can think of is that my eyes hurt. Hey, is that your mother home already?"

Zoe jumped up when she heard the kitchen door slam and began to fold the newspaper. "Go talk to her, Ruthie. I have to get this out of the paper before Daddy sees it. Boy, it's a good thing you wanted to read 'Dear Abby.' If Daddy had seen the announcement first . . ."

Ruthie ran for the kitchen and Zoe crossed the hall to her father's study. She decided to cut out the whole page, rather than risk her father's questions about a suspicious hole. After she stuffed the page in her jumper pocket and replaced the clipping scissors beside the typewriter, she put the paper on the front porch again and strolled into the kitchen.

Her mother was slumped at the kitchen table, with her shoes off and her feet up on a chair, talking to Ruthie. Her school books and papers lay on the floor beside her purse.

As Zoe entered, Ruthie was saying, "Mrs. Edwards, do you like pets?"

Zoe made frantic shushing motions behind her mother's back. Sometimes Ruthie was about as subtle as a plane wreck, and just as disastrous.

"Pets? Why?" Mrs. Edwards's eyebrows went up. She had three children of her own and a whole kindergarten class to cope with, and she knew better than to answer a sudden irrelevant question.

Zoe interrupted hastily. "Hi, Mother. Want your tea?"

"Hi, dear. Yes, please. I'm just exhausted. Those kids get worse every year."

"You just think so because you're getting older," Ruthie said comfortingly. "There's more of a generation gap."

Mrs. Edwards's eyebrows went up again. "Is that so? Well, I'll tell you, Ruthie, the only time I'm happy about teaching five-year-olds is when I consider what a certain person's fifth-grade class must be like!"

"You mean me?" Ruthie inquired innocently. "Mrs. Hannum says we're at a delightful age."

"Mrs. Hannum has obviously been teaching too long," said Mrs. Edwards. She watched Zoe pour hot water into her cup and said, "What's for dinner? Check the schedule, will you, Zoe?"

"Oh, let me," said Ruthie, jumping up while Zoe poured her tea. "I love to read your schedules." She went to the crowded bulletin board beside the stove and ran her finger down a long strip of adding-machine tape.

Mrs. Edwards had only one rule for her family, but it was an all-inclusive one: Follow the schedule. She had schedules for everything. On the bulletin board were shopping schedules, chore schedules, cleaning schedules, homework, entertainment, and birthday schedules, all made out on adding-machine tape and running for three months. When a schedule ran out, she took a day off from kindergarten, stayed in bed all day, and made out a new one.

Anyone in the Edwards house who didn't follow the schedule was in trouble. Zoe tried, but sometimes forgot, and sometimes couldn't get all the chores done. Bob, who was a senior, always did his ahead of time. Marcia, a year younger than Bob, had traded so many days with Zoe that no one was sure whether she did her part or not.

Mr. Edwards's name never appeared on the schedule.

Now Ruthie found Tuesday on the menu schedule and read, "Meat loaf. Eccck! Can I come to dinner on Saturday? Lasagna! Yummy!"

Zoe took a foil-wrapped package out of the freezer and slid it into the oven. Mrs. Edwards watched her set the dial and said suspiciously, "Why are you being so helpful? It's not your turn to do dinner, is it?"

"Marcia called. She's at the library with Roger. We traded days."

"Seems to me you two are doing a lot of trading lately. This never happened when Hershel was around." She sipped her tea thoughtfully and watched Zoe open cans. "I don't know about this new boy."

Ruthie sprinkled cinnamon sugar in her tea. "Roger? He's neat-o!"

Zoe wrapped foil around four potatoes and said, "Oh,

Ruthie, you think anything in pants is neat-o. I can't *stand* Roger!"

"Neither can your father," said Mrs. Edwards. "He misses all those good political arguments with Hershel when he came to see Marcia."

"Doesn't Hershel come to see Bob?" asked Ruthie. "I mean, just because he stopped dating Marcia is no reason to give up his best friend."

"They go out to the garage workshop, or up in Bob's room to talk," said Zoe. "He doesn't even come to borrow books from Daddy anymore."

Zoe sat down at the table with her mother and Ruthie just as the front door slammed. She and Ruthie looked at each other. Zoe fingered the newspaper page in her pocket. She held her breath as she heard another door open and close — the closet. Then another — the study. She breathed again.

"Hershel's mistake," Ruthie went on, "was the beard."

Mrs. Edwards laughed. "That may have been the last straw. But Marcia didn't like the sandals or the long hair, either. Or picketing the school for a meditation day. Is he still practicing Zen, I wonder?"

"Marcia's smart," said Ruthie. "Would you rather sit around and argue politics and talk about *books*, or go to the country-club dance?"

"I don't know how smart she is," said Zoe. "Hershel's fun."

"Marcia just got tired of waiting for him and your father to finish their conversations," said Mrs. Edwards. She giggled. "Sometimes they never got out of the house at all on a date."

Ruthie was so horrified she forgot to chew her gum.

"Well, I'd never let a boy do me that way. A girl has to be practical." She finished her tea, put down her cup, and informed them, "Hershel's a kook. Kooks are fun to know — but not to date."

Mrs. Edwards laughed. "Ruthie, I'm glad you're not old enough for a boy friend. If you ever get rid of that bubble gum, you'll give the boys a hard time, I'll bet."

"I intend to," said Ruthie. "But I can't give up gum. It helps me think."

Suddenly, from the front of the house, came a muffled rumble. Zoe and Ruthie looked at each other across the table and waited. A door flew open. The rumble grew to a roar. Then the mean-old-man-of-the-mountain bellowed, "Who's been cutting up my newspaper?"

"How did he know?" Zoe whispered.

"Psychic," said Ruthie, and headed for the kitchen door. "See you, Zoe! Remember — logic!"

"Wait! You're forgetting your notebook — and your coat!"

The door slammed. "I don't know what you two have been up to, but you look guilty," said Mrs. Edwards. "Get in there and find out what's wrong, Zoe. And don't expect me to be peacemaker. I'm too tired."

Touching the newspaper page stuffed in her pocket, Zoe tiptoed through the hall to the cave of the mean-old-man-of-the-mountain.

2

LONG AGO ZOE's mother had removed the study from her cleaning schedule. The last time she had vacuumed in there, she often recalled, was two years ago when Mr.

Edwards went to San Francisco for the Modern Language Association convention.

If someone moved a single stack of the pamphlets, yellowing newspaper clippings, or moldering letters that carpeted the floor, Mr. Edwards merely growled and muttered. But anyone foolish enough to touch one of the sacred folders, papers, or notes that were miscellaneously categorized by his children as Daddy's Important Work, risked being thrown bodily from the room.

Zoe peeked through the study door and saw her father enthroned beside the fireplace in his wicker rocking chair. He was muttering to himself, scowling, and turning the pages of the newspaper furiously. When he saw Zoe, he shoved his glasses high on his forehead and waved the paper at her.

"Are you the idiot that cut out the editorial page? Where is it?"

"Editorial page?" Zoe had a sinking feeling that she should have looked on the back of the page she cut out. "Is there something important tonight?"

"Important! This paper hasn't said anything important since the Civil War, when they *did* come out against slavery, surprisingly. But I may have a letter to the editor printed tonight. Where's the page?"

Zoe stalled. "*Another* letter? Will we get some more of those funny phone calls from people who don't like it?"

"Quacks! That's what they are. Don't know good sense when they read it. Come on, Zoe, get me the paper. I have Important Work to do."

There was nothing to do but pull it from her jumper pocket. It only tore a little when she unfolded it.

Mr. Edwards held the page between thumb and forefinger and looked at it as if she had just handed him the garbage. He waved it incredulously before her. "What's the meaning of this?" he spluttered. "How am I supposed to read anything in this condition? How many times have I told you . . . What's this? What's this?"

He had seen it.

Zoe chewed on her braid as he read the announcement once, frowned at her, pulled his glasses down from his forehead and read it again. She knew exactly what he would say, and he did.

"Ye gods!"

"Did you find your editorial page, dear?" asked Mrs. Edwards from the doorway.

"Helen, come in here and read this. Don't step on those papers!"

Mrs. Edwards picked her way across the room, hopping from one bare spot to another. She perched on the arm of the sofa, the only spot not covered with old newspapers, and smoothed the page out on top of a stack of books on the table in front of her.

Looking over her shoulder, Zoe read the announcement again:

ZUCCINI'S ZODIAC

A Circle of Pets from Around the Universe!!!

Grand Opening

Free Goldfish!!   Refreshments!!

Saturday, January 23

Meet the Winner of the Zodiac Contest!!

MISS ZOE EDWARDS
43 College Hill Road

"You won a contest!" said her mother. "How nice! What did you win?"

"What kind of contest?" Mr. Edwards asked. "Explain. And get your foot off that folder. Sit."

Zoe looked around for a place to sit and finally perched on the *Webster's Third International* on the hearth. "It's a long story," she said. "Maybe I ought to do my homework first."

"Now, Zoe. I'm behind schedule," said her mother. "Why are you avoiding us? You should be congratulated!"

Zoe reached for the end of her braid, noticed it had dust on it from dangling on the hearth, and brushed it off. Then she changed her mind, clasped her hands around her knees, and began.

"Back in November, when I had that big history project, remember, I had to go to the library practically every day. I always stopped at the bakery on the way, and I started watching some workmen remodeling the shop next door. One day there was a big sign in the window announcing that it was going to be a pet shop called Zuccini's Zodiac. And next time I went by, there was a big round poster about the contest."

She stopped to make herself more comfortable on the dictionary. "It was a circle of animals," she went on, "and anybody who wanted to could try to guess what they were."

"Were they signs of the zodiac, you mean?" asked Mrs. Edwards.

Zoe shook her head. "No, no. They weren't like Pisces or Taurus or any of those. They were *unusual* animals."

"Such as?" her father asked.

"Well, there was a peregrine falcon, and a duck-billed platypus, and a brachiopod — "

"That's a rock," her father interrupted.

"Fossil, maybe," Zoe corrected. "A brachiopod is any

mollusklike, marine animal of the phylum *brachiopoda,* having a dorsal and ventral shell."

"Ye gods!"

"But how did you *know* that, Zoe?" asked Mrs. Edwards.

"I was going to the library anyway. Every day I looked up one. Then I got an entry blank and sent it in."

"And you won!" said her mother. She bent over the paper again. "What did you win? The paper just says 'Zodiac Contest.'"

"That's what I won."

"Explain," said Mr. Edwards.

Zoe squirmed on her dictionary. "Well, a zodiac is — "

"I know what a zodiac is," Mr. Edwards said impatiently. "From the Greek, 'circle of animals.'"

"Well," said Zoe, taking a deep breath and picking up her dusty braid, "that's what I won."

Mrs. Edwards's eyebrows were way up. "A circle of animals, one for each month of the year. A circle — oh, Zoe, surely you didn't — "

Miserably, Zoe nodded.

"*Twelve animals?*"

"Twelve."

"Twelve!" Mr. Edwards exploded. He bounded out of his chair and began to pace the floor, stepping over mounds of papers and books as he went. "Twelve! Twelve animals is a menagerie, a zoo. Do you mean to say somebody with a name like a vegetable is going to come driving a herd of twelve animals across my lawn? Because if that's what you're saying — "

"No, no, Daddy! You don't understand."

Mr. Edwards stopped just short of a mountain of *New*

York Times Book Reviews. "What? What?"

"It's like a real zodiac," Zoe explained. "It takes a year. One pet for each new sign of the zodiac."

"Ye gods! A pet-of-the-month club, yet!"

Zoe laughed. "Oh, Daddy, that's a good one!"

He stopped again and glared at her. "Don't be sarcastic."

"But I'm not — "

He resumed his pacing. "I can see it all now," he muttered, making a right turn at the drama bookshelf. "Apes in the attic, peacocks on the porch, orangutans in the outhouse — "

"Outhouse!" exclaimed Mrs. Edwards.

"Figuratively speaking," he said, halting by the typewriter table. "This is ridiculous, Zoe. One pet, perhaps. But twelve? Impossible! I commend you for doing the research and winning the contest, but you simply cannot accept such a prize. After school tomorrow you call this — what's his name?"

"Zuccini. He's Italian. He looks like — "

" — Zuccini and tell him the situation." And as if that ended that, he settled in his rocker and picked up the newspaper.

"Why can't I have them, Daddy?"

He pushed up his glasses. "Why? That is the most ridiculous question I've heard today. Where would we *put* twelve animals?"

"Daddy, he's not going to give away apes and orangutans! Just *little* things that won't take any space or be any trouble. That's only logical. And this is a big house! And we have a yard, and a garage, and — "

Mr. Edwards sighed and put down his paper. "How

could we feed them? Your brother eats enough during basketball season to put us in the poorhouse. I can't afford to buy fodder for the entire cast of the ark!"

"I'll buy the food. With my allowance."

"Ha!" He picked up his paper. "No, Zoe, we won't discuss it anymore."

He went back to his newspaper, ignoring her as she sat slumped on the big dictionary. Zoe widened her eyes and stared at a pile of old *Time* magazines. The aroma of baking meat loaf drifted in from the kitchen. Zoe thought about the starving children in Africa. She sniffed loudly enough to get her father's attention as a tear rolled down her face.

Mrs. Edwards's eyebrows went up as she looked at her daughter. Muttering something about meat loaf, she fled.

"Stop that!" said Mr. Edwards. "There's nothing to cry about."

Zoe sniffed again, sighed, and dragged herself up off the dictionary and to the door, where she stopped and looked back at her father.

"If *you* won a nice prize, you wouldn't let anybody take it away from you," she told him.

When she reported to Ruthie on the upstairs phone, Ruthie had a few more ideas. "Not bad for the first round," she said. "Now the next thing you have to do is get Marcia and Bob on your side. And then . . ."

3

HUDDLED IN HER RED COAT on the front steps, Zoe waited for her brother to come home from basketball practice.

The streetlight in front of the house was glowing in the early winter darkness before she saw him come jogging down the street. He turned up the front walk and stopped before her.

"Hello, Abominable Snowman. What did you do this time?"

"I had to t-t-talk to you before d-d-dinner," Zoe said.

"Well, stand up and jog. You'll freeze."

Zoe stood up and pulled the crumpled newspaper page from her pocket.

"You want me to read? Jog down here under the streetlight."

They jogged in place under the streetlight while Bob read. Zoe thought if anyone could talk her father into the pets, Bob could. Mr. Edwards never yelled at Bob. He listened. Somewhat in awe of his tall son's ability to unclog drains and fix broken toasters as well as play basketball and earn all his own money, Mr. Edwards respected Bob's opinion on anything.

Zoe herself thought Bob the best brother anyone could have. He was always ready to advance a loan until Saturday or patch a bicycle tire. And he was nothing at all like Marcia.

Bob was reading the announcement aloud as the red Mustang pulled up to the curb.

"Are you two out of your minds?" Marcia asked as she climbed out. "No, don't get out, Roger. It's too cold. See you in French tomorrow."

Zoe immediately jogged in a half circle until her back was to the Mustang. She hoped Roger noticed. Bob, however, went over to the car and spoke to Roger.

From inside the car, Roger said, " 'Night, Marcia. Bob,

old boy, if you need exercise, why don't you take up basketball? Ha, ha!"

Zoe made a face at the car as it pulled away from the curb.

"Wait a minute, Marcia," said Bob, as his sister turned toward the house. "Read this."

"Are you out of your mind?" Marcia asked again. "I'm not reading anything out here. It's freezing."

"Please, Marcia," said Zoe. "I need your help. I did you a favor."

"Oh, speaking of favors, Zoe," said Marcia, her tone changing to the loving-sister one, "will you do my chores Saturday? Roger asked me to the game and to his brother's fraternity party! Isn't that nice?"

"Sure," said Zoe, so quickly that Marcia's eyes narrowed. "Jog, and you'll keep warm. And read this."

She read, after putting her books down on the sidewalk. "You won a contest! What did you win?"

Zoe explained, puffing a little from the exercise. As she told them, Bob's grin widened, but Marcia's frown deepened.

"A pet a month for a year? You're goofy. And Daddy will have a fit."

"He already had it. That's why I need help."

"I think," said Bob, "that Zoe wants us to put up a united front."

"Well, count me out," Marcia said, her voice determined. "I refuse to turn this place into a farm. It's junky enough as it is."

"Our house isn't junky!" said Zoe. She wouldn't live anywhere else but in the big old Victorian house, white frame, trimmed with what was called gingerbread. She had

grown up there and she loved it. It was Marcia's new boy
friend, Zoe knew, who was turning her against such an
old-fashioned home. Zoe had seen Roger's house. It was
mostly glass.

Zoe's braid bobbed up and down as she jogged faster.
"I just remembered. I'm going to be busy Saturday. In
fact, I'm going to be busy just about every day from now
on."

Marcia stopped jogging. "That's blackmail!"

"That's bargaining," said Zoe.

"Who's *that?*" asked Bob.

A white panel truck stopped beside them, and a man
got out. He was short and round and smiling. He wore
no overcoat, but a dark blue jacket with many pockets,
flaps, and buttons, which sparkled in the light. Above his
beautiful teeth was a curling, droopy mustache. He wore
a jaunty red beret, which he removed as he walked toward
them. On his shoulder rode a tiny brown monkey, his long
brown tail wrapped around the man's neck.

Zoe, of course, knew who he was before he said a word.
She said, "Hello, Mr. Zuccini. I'm Zoe. This is my brother
Bob and my sister Marcia."

As Mr. Zuccini flourished his beret in front of his
paunch and bowed low before Marcia, the monkey almost
fell off his shoulder.

"I am honored!" the pet-store owner boomed in a deep
Italian basso. He raised Marcia's mittened hand to his
lips and kissed it tenderly. "Never expected to see such
charming lady tonight."

Marcia was enchanted. She held up her hand limply
and gazed at the mitten. Mr. Zuccini shook Bob's hand

vigorously. The monkey on his shoulder bounced up and down and clung to his ear.

"And you are Zoe," Mr. Zuccini said. "I am so glad! Every day I see you stand in front of shop and eat dough-nut and look at poster. I hope when I read contest entries that little girl with long pigtail win. And you did. Congratulations!" He shook her hand and then bowed, too. The monkey hung on.

"Don't congratulate her yet, Mr. Zuccini," said Bob. "We have a little problem. You'd better jog while we tell you about it."

Five minutes later, when Mr. Edwards peered out the front door to see if the snow had started again, he was amazed to see, in the circle of light cast by the streetlamp, his three children, an Italian organ grinder and a monkey, all bobbing up and down like jumping jacks. Little frosty balloons appeared before their faces and disappeared.

"Helen, come here!" he yelled, and his wife hurried in-to the hall, the dinner gong and clapper in her hand. As they watched, the strange quartet turned toward the house and jogged single file up the steps and into the hall.

"Mother and Daddy," said Zoe breathlessly, "this is Mr. Zuccini. Can he stay for dinner?"

Mr. and Mrs. Edwards stared as if hypnotized at the monkey, who stared back with round, liquid eyes. Mrs. Edwards recovered first. "Please be our guest, Mr. Zuccini, if you don't mind a simple dinner. Zoe, run and set another place."

Mr. Edwards pointed to the monkey. "That's not — surely, that's not — "

Mr. Zuccini lifted the monkey off his shoulder, threw back his head, and laughed. "No, no! This not for Zoe.

This is Dante. He gets lonesome in shop. Likes to come along with me."

"Oh," said Mr. Edwards, and let out his breath.

The Edwards family never ate in their dining room, which was huge and dark and filled with massive, old-fashioned oak furniture that had been in the house for fifty years. They led Mr. Zuccini through the kitchen to the room on the other side, which everyone except Marcia called the breakfast room. Marcia called it the family room, which Mr. Edwards said was too suburban. The room contained not only the table where they ate, but also a sofa and chairs, a desk, the television set, and a fireplace. Mr. Zuccini loved it.

"Wonderful house!" he boomed as he deposited the monkey on a bookshelf. "Always I admire old houses, with — what you call it? — gingerbread trimming, and the tower — "

"It's a turret," said Zoe. "Can Dante have a banana?"

"You wouldn't like fixing all the things that go wrong in a big house," said Mr. Edwards, serving the green beans.

Marcia giggled. "Daddy can't fix a broken pencil, Mr. Zuccini. Bob's the handyman. The heaviest work Daddy does is lift a volume of Shakespeare."

"Shakespeare!" Mr. Zuccini exclaimed. "You literary man, Mr. Edwards?"

"Daddy teaches at the college," Marcia explained. "And writes letters to the editor."

"Meat loaf again?" asked Mr. Edwards, as his wife passed him the plate. "Didn't we just have that?"

"We have not had meat loaf," answered his wife sweetly, with her eyebrows raised, "since Wednesday, December nineteenth. Check the schedule."

"Meat loaf!" said Mr. Zuccini. "Mrs. Edwards, this is feast! Banquet! I never get such wonderful food!"

Mrs. Edwards heaped his plate, asking, "Isn't there a *Mrs.* Zuccini?"

"Alas, no! I have no charming wife, no tall son, no beautiful daughters." He made little bows all around the table as he spoke. "You must work all day on such a magnificent meal, Mrs. Edwards. Delicious!"

"Oh, no," said Zoe. "Mother teaches kindergarten. She's out all day."

"What! I can hardly believe it! Such organization! Wonderful!"

Mrs. Edwards was enchanted. She filled his plate again.

"Are you ready for your grand opening, Mr. Zuccini?" asked Bob.

"Almost. Animals arriving every day. You come to grand opening, Zoe? Got to have your picture made with first pet, you know, for newspaper. Good publicity. You serve punch and goldfish, too!"

Zoe looked at her father, who was frowning, picking at his meat loaf with his fork.

"Mr. Zuccini, I think we might as well get this settled before it goes any further. We have decided that Zoe should not accept your prize. We — "

"Who's decided?" asked Bob.

"Nobody asked me," said Marcia, after Zoe kicked her under the table.

Mr. and Mrs. Edwards looked at each of them and then at each other. Mrs. Edwards smiled. "They're right, dear. It was *your* decision. Nobody asked *me* about it, either."

"You know, Mr. Edwards, that I would not give Zoe a

pet hard to care for, or expensive to feed," said Mr. Zuccini. He clapped his big hand to his chest. "Believe me!"

"What — what sort of pets did you have in mind, then?" asked Mr. Edwards.

"Ah, can't tell *what!*" Mr. Zuccini winked at Zoe. "Surprise is half the fun."

"Zoe can't take care of her own room," said Mrs. Edwards slowly, "much less twelve animals. I was up there yesterday looking for spoons and the place looked like a United Nations rummage sale."

"Spoons? Spoons?" asked Mr. Edwards. "Why were you looking for spoons in Zoe's room?"

Mrs. Edwards got up to clear the table. "She takes snacks up and never brings back the dishes."

Zoe slid down in her chair as her mother removed her plate. "I meant to clean it up. I just didn't have time!"

"Time! You never have time for anything that's work. Such as practicing." Mrs. Edwards disappeared into the kitchen.

"Practicing what?" asked Mr. Zuccini.

"Piano," said Zoe. "I hate it."

Mr. Zuccini's black eyes widened and he tore his napkin from the neck of his jacket. "What! I can't believe my ears! You have chance to play *instrument* and you not practice!"

Mr. Edwards looked at him and smiled broadly.

Mr. Zuccini went on. "All my life, when I was a child in Milano, growing up in three rooms, ten of us, I dream of someday having books, music, art, fine house! Never want a million dollars, just good life! And now I see you, growing up in house like I always want, and you — you *not practice!*"

Zoe slid so far down in her chair that her chin was level with the table.

Mr. Zuccini mopped his brow with his napkin. "Sorry, Zoe. Got carried away. Didn't mean to shout at you."

Mrs. Edwards came back from the kitchen carrying a tray of dessert. "*And,*" she said, "because Zoe is so bad about cleaning her room — "

"Not to mention the multiplication tables," interrupted Mr. Edwards.

"Multiplication tables?" asked Mr. Zuccini.

"She can't multiply," said Mr. Edwards. "My daughter. Ten years old and she won't say the multiplication tables until she knows them."

"As I was saying," said Mrs. Edwards, putting Mr. Zuccini's ice cream before him, "because Zoe is so bad about things, I think it might be a good idea if she accepted a little responsibility. Like pets."

Zoe breathed again and sat up straight.

Bob spoke for the first time and all heads turned to him. "Exactly. Let Zoe have the pets. But on approval."

"Approval?" asked his father. "Approval? Like stamps?"

"If she doesn't do her jobs, the pets go back."

Everyone digested this with his ice cream. "Fair enough," decided Mrs. Edwards. "And Zoe — "

"No," said Mr. Edwards.

"Oh, come on, Dad."

"Be a pussy cat, Daddy!"

Zoe ate her ice cream and thought of the mammoths trapped in the glaciers. A little tear appeared beside her nose. Her father stopped his spoon halfway to his mouth and looked at her suspiciously.

"So, Zoe," said Mr. Zuccini, "you agree to keep room clean?"

Zoe sniffed and nodded her head until her braid bounced.

"Say the multiplication tables every day and practice the music?"

Zoe nodded more slowly.

"Take care of all pets?"

"Oh, yes!"

"One more thing you have to do, Zoe," said Mr. Zuccini. He wagged his finger at Zoe, frowned, and spoke slowly and seriously. "Must never, *never let pets disturb your father*. Never! Your father is scholar, professor, author!"

Mr. Edwards looked pleased. He almost smiled. Mr. Zuccini continued.

"Your father does most important work in world, children!" he said, standing up and putting his big hand over his heart. "Anybody can learn to fix broken things, cook magnificent meals, look lovely, even multiply!" He bowed around the table again as he spoke. "But only man of great learning can teach, write, create! Must respect your father! Never let *anything* disturb his Important Work!"

Mr. Edwards was enchanted.

4

OPENING A pet shop was hard work, Zoe found.

Tired and hungry, Zoe climbed down from the white panel truck and waved until it rounded the corner in the dark. She clutched her package to her coat and walked slowly up the steps. She had poured gallons of pink punch all day and given away two hundred goldfish in plastic bags.

She smelled the lasagna as she opened the door. Her father was in the study, she saw as she went toward the kitchen, muttering and turning pages of his paper. Zoe considered showing her pet to him, since he was apparently finding something in the paper to make him mad, which always put him in a good mood. Then he chuckled, and she changed her mind.

Mrs. Edwards looked up from the salad she was tossing as Zoe entered the kitchen. "Hello, dear. You're just in time. Have a good day?"

"Great! But I'm glad I don't have to open a pet shop every day." Zoe put her package on the kitchen table. Marcia and Bob came in from the breakfast room as they heard her voice.

Marcia pointed to the little package, which was wrapped in red paper with black zodiac signs on it. "What's in the box?"

"My pet," Zoe said, and began to tear off the paper.

Mrs. Edwards put down the spoons and came to watch as Zoe lifted a small matchstick-bamboo cage by its carrying handle.

"How darling!" said Marcia. "It looks like my summer purse."

"It's a cricket cage," Zoe told her.

"Oh, I'm so relieved," said Mrs. Edwards. "Your father was expecting at least apes or peacocks."

"Where's the bug?" asked Marcia, peering through the delicate bars.

"Insect, not bug," said Zoe. "I thought you didn't like bugs."

"Oh, he can't be too bad if he lives in this cute little house." Marcia took the cage from Zoe and turned it around in her hands. "Oh, look, there's a little door. How does it — "

Suddenly a small, dark object went hurtling through the air, landed on the floor, and hopped in three quick motions across the room. Before anyone could move, it had disappeared under the stove.

Marcia stood looking helplessly at the cage, her face stricken. Bob was already stretched out in front of the stove, trying to see under it.

"We'll never find him," Zoe wailed. "I just know we won't."

"No hysterics, Zoe," said Bob. "We'll get him. Find me something to put over him to trap him. And the flashlight."

Suddenly, from under the stove came a CHIRRRRUP!

"He's getting warm," said Zoe.

"I sure am," Bob muttered. "What are you cooking in here, anyway? Pottery?"

"I mean the cricket's getting warmer. That's why he sings." Zoe handed Bob the flashlight from the everything drawer.

CHIRRRUP! CHIRRRUP!

"Count how many times he chirps in fifteen seconds and add thirty-nine," said Zoe. "You can tell the temperature that way."

Bob raised himself on one elbow and looked at her as if she were demented. "Will you please hand me *something* to catch him under."

"Well, Mr. Zuccini said you could tell the temperature," she said defensively.

Marcia snatched the first lid she saw from the kitchen counter and handed it to Bob. "I hope he likes Thousand Island dressing," she said.

Bob aimed the flashlight beam under the stove and slid one long arm underneath. There was a little click as he dropped the lid over the cricket. Zoe watched anxiously as he began to move backward, dragging the lid with the cricket trapped underneath with him.

"Gather around me," he said. "Be ready to grab him as I take the lid off. Zoe, get the cage."

Mrs. Edwards, Zoe, and Marcia knelt around Bob, ready to cup hands over the cricket as Bob slowly lifted the lid. Marcia said, "I hope he doesn't hop to me."

"You let him out," said Bob. "You have to help." He lifted the lid.

Underneath was an enormous black cockroach.

Marcia screamed and fled blindly toward the breakfast room. Mrs. Edwards climbed to the top of the kitchen stool and began yelling for bug spray. Zoe scooted sideways so the innocent cockroach could scuttle back to darkness and sanity. Bob lay on the floor with his head in his arms, his shoulders shaking with silent laughter.

Mr. Edwards ran into the room, trailing newspaper pages. "Ye gods! Who screamed? What happened? Is he hurt?"

"It's only my pet, Daddy," said Zoe.

"Pet? Pet? *What did your pet do to my son?* Why is he lying there?"

"Get the bug spray!" yelled Mrs. Edwards.

Bob rolled over, very much alive and unhurt, and explained the situation to his father. Marcia was coaxed back into the room and Mrs. Edwards persuaded them that they couldn't spray until both the cricket and the lasagna were out. But there still remained the problem of the cricket, who chirped happily in his warm home.

"Couldn't we save the cage and find another one this summer?" suggested Marcia. "All right, all right, it was just an idea."

"I think they're attracted to light," said Zoe. "That's where you usually see them in the summer. Let's put the

flashlight by the stove and see if he'll crawl out to it."

"Good idea," said Bob. "Marcia can keep watch."

"Me!"

"You let him out, dear sister."

It took a while. Marcia finished her plate of lasagna, sitting cross-legged in front of the stove, and had begun her ice cream when she whispered loudly, "Zoe! He's coming out!"

Everyone except Mr. Edwards left his dessert and rushed into the kitchen.

Moving his jointed legs in slow motion, wiggling his antennae backward, the small brown insect crawled toward the beam of light. Marcia scooted backward as he came, and Zoe bent forward with her hands cupped, scooped up the cricket, and deposited him tenderly in the bamboo cage.

She took the cage to show her father, who was calmly spooning up ice cream in the breakfast room. He peered through the bars of the cage and said, "Well, I suppose he's little enough to be harmless."

Mrs. Edwards went to put on the water for her tea. "Have you cleaned your room, Zoe?" she called from the kitchen.

"Almost. There was a little — accumulation. But I'm almost done."

"Let me know if you find my asparagus tongs," her mother called. "I haven't seen them since Christmas and I'll bet they're under your bed."

CHIRRUP! CHIRRUP! CHIRRUP! CHIRRUP! CHIRRUP!

Zoe jumped up. "What's wrong with him?"

"Must be two hundred degrees in here," answered Bob.

The cricket went on and on, drowning out the sound of the teakettle. Mr. Edwards, scraping the last of his ice cream from the dish, said, "Turn off the teakettle. He'll stop."

He did.

"Daddy," said Zoe, "sometimes I think you're smarter than we know."

Mr. Edwards smiled smugly. "If you'd read a book now and then, you'd learn about crickets."

"I read a whole chapter in one of the books at the pet shop," said Zoe, "and they don't say a *thing* about tea-kettles."

"I'm thinking of Dickens. *The Cricket on the Hearth.* There is a cricket in there which has a contest with a tea-kettle."

"Our gas stove is hardly a hearth!" said Mrs. Edwards. "Nevertheless, I think he's very cheerful to have around. Zoe, may we keep him in the kitchen?"

Zoe had wanted him in her bedroom, but she thought it best to let her mother put it wherever she wanted to.

"Aren't they good luck?" asked Marcia.

Mr. Edwards nodded. "To have a cricket on the hearth, 'tis the luckiest thing in all the world."

"What was Dickens's first name?" asked Zoe.

"Charles."

"Then let's call him Charlie Cricket."

Bob said, "It beats Jiminy."

"I'll bet Mr. Zuccini knows crickets are good luck," said Zoe. "That's why he made that the first pet."

Mr. Edwards smiled. "I think he might have had another motive," he said. "And let me tell you, young lady, that lonesome monkey act didn't fool me. I know very well what he meant to do with that monkey, until you three plotted something under that streetlight."

Marcia and Zoe and Bob looked at each other.

"Daddy," said Zoe, "sometimes I *know* you're smarter than we think."

PISCES

●

February 20 – March 20

1

THE FRONT PORCH of the Edwards house curved around the conical turret at the corner and then extended the full length of the side, along the living room. It was an excellent place to practice cartwheels on a mild February Saturday.

Zoe and Ruthie whirled head over heels until they were out of breath and then climbed on the banister to rest. Hooking her heels through the elaborate woodwork and leaning against the post, Zoe asked, "When is the gym program, anyway?"

"Two weeks. And I'm scared!"

"Why? We have two weeks to practice. All we have to do is turn cartwheels around the stage to end the program. Think of all those guys in the human pyramid."

Ruthie's bubble burst on her nose. "All I can think of is all those cute sixth-grade boys out front watching me. I'll just die!"

"You'll love it, and you know it," said Zoe. "Honestly Ruthie, you are the most boy-crazy girl in the fifth grade. What are you going to be like in high school with all those boys?"

"I don't know," said Ruthie dreamily, "but I can hardly wait." She stared off into space and then sat up so quickly she nearly fell off the banister into the hedge. Zoe turned to see what she had seen.

Hershel was shuffling up the sidewalk. He was wrapped in a rather moldy black cloak, which fell almost to his sandals. His sandy beard had grown spectacularly, as had his hair. He took off his dark glasses and waved at them as he came up the walk.

"Hi, Hershel," said Ruthie. "Aren't your feet cold?"

Hershel grinned, yanked on Zoe's braid, and straddled the banister beside them. "Nope. Got more important things to think of than the weather. Bob home, Zoe?"

"Upstairs. And Marcia's in the breakfast room with her face *covered* with cream and her hair up in curlers, so be careful."

"Let's go in," said Ruthie. "She'd jump a mile if Hershel saw her."

Hershel shook his head sadly. "Be kind, ladies. We aren't meant for each other. Our stars are crossed."

"Had any good meditations lately?" asked Ruthie.

Hershel shook his shaggy head again, sadly. "I've given it up, Ruthie. I gave myself until last Sunday to achieve Nirvana, and I didn't, so I quit."

"What have you taken up now?" asked Zoe. "I *know* you're doing something funny. You always are."

"Funny! Astrology certainly isn't funny. It's a very serious science."

Ruthie stopped in mid-bubble. "Can you tell horoscopes?"

"*Cast* horoscopes, Ruthie, *cast*. I am getting to be an expert. What are you?"

"You mean what sign? A crab."

"Just what I always suspected. Zoe?"

"I think — Gemini. Is that June?"

"Right. O.K., girls, I'll work on it." Hershel swung his leg over the banister and went inside. As the door closed after him, a familiar white truck pulled into the driveway. Zoe and Ruthie jumped off the porch over the hedge and ran across the lawn to meet Mr. Zuccini. He was opening the back of the truck and unloading a large, apparently heavy, square package, which was wrapped in the red and black zodiac paper.

"Hi, Zoe! And you, I bet, are Ruthie. How do you do, Ruthie?" He put down the package again so he could bow to Ruthie, who held out her hand, expectantly. Mr. Zuccini grinned and bestowed a kiss on it.

Zoe's eyes were on the package. "You picked a good day to bring it," she told Mr. Zuccini. "Daddy's not home. Can I help you carry it?"

"I manage," he puffed, staggering up the steps. "How's cricket?"

Zoe held open the front door for him. "Fine! Sings all the time and he *loves* corn flakes."

Marcia, who was curled in a corner of the sofa painting her nails with silver polish, squealed when they came in the breakfast room. She jumped up and tried to hide the pink curlers and the blue face cream without getting her nails damaged.

"Oh, Zoe, how *could* you bring someone in here!" she said. "I'm so embarrassed." She fled toward the door.

"We didn't come to see you anyway," said Ruthie. "And you better not go upstairs. Hershel's up there."

Marcia stopped in her tracks. Mr. Zuccini had put the package down on the table before the sofa, and now he swept off his beret and bowed gallantly, completely ignoring the curlers and the cream and the old blue jeans. Marcia sat down on the couch again, glaring at Zoe, who was tearing the paper off the package.

It was a terrarium, partly filled with soil and plants. Ruthie and Marcia, who forgot her appearance for a minute, bent over it.

"Where is it?" asked Ruthie.

"*What* is it?" asked Marcia.

"It's a chameleon," said Zoe, tapping with her finger on the side nearest her. "See? On the twig."

Looking closely, they could see the chameleon put out a fantastically long tongue, slither off the twig and under a leaf.

"He's changing colors," said Ruthie. "He was gray and now he's green."

Marcia shivered delicately. "It looks like a miniature monster. Don't let it near me!"

"He won't hurt you," Ruthie assured her. "My brother used to have one. He used to put him in the girls' hair."

Marcia moved back a little from the terrarium.

"What does he eat?" asked Zoe.

"Here — I have food somewhere." Mr. Zuccini opened

a few flaps and found a box of food in a pocket of his blue jacket. "Of course, you get insects live for him in summer. He is great hunter."

Marcia giggled. "Put the cricket in there, Zoe. Yummy!"

"My brother used to let his have gigantic bugs to fight with," said Ruthie. "Pick him up, Zoe. My brother used to let his ride on his shoulder."

Zoe looked questioningly at Mr. Zuccini, who nodded. The chameleon allowed Zoe to pick him up.

"See, he's changing colors," said Ruthie, when the chameleon was on Zoe's shoulder, three inches from her chin. "Poke him, Zoe, so he'll change again." She jabbed at the lizard with her forefinger.

Zoe jumped back. "Stop that! How would you like to be poked so you'd change colors?" She poked Ruthie hard in the stomach.

"Ow! You don't have to get nasty! It doesn't hurt them. My brother used to do it all the time."

"You sure changed colors, Ruthie," said Marcia.

"You don't have to walk so carefully," said Mr. Zuccini, as Zoe took a few tentative steps. "He won't fall off."

"My brother tied a string around the neck of his chameleon and pinned it to his pocket," said Ruthie. "He used to wear him to school."

"Really?" said Zoe. "Didn't it hurt the chameleon?"

"Oh, no. You can jump up and down with him and everything. My brother did it all the time. Once he even cut off his tail to see if it would really grow back."

Zoe was horrified and looked it. "Well, *did* it grow back?"

"No," Ruthie admitted.

"What finally happened to your brother's chameleon?" asked Marcia.

Ruthie blew a bubble while she thought. When it smashed on her nose, she said, "I really don't remember. It died. But I forget how."

Coming into the hall to say good-bye, Zoe, Ruthie, and Mr. Zuccini saw first Hershel's sandals, then the black cloak, and then the beard, as he came down the stairs from Bob's room. Mr. Zuccini stared open-mouthed at him.

"Who's the hippie?" he whispered loudly to Zoe.

"It's only Hershel," said Zoe. "He's not a hippie. He dresses that way because his counselor told him he was insecure and he should practice being in the spotlight so he could lose his shyness."

"All he lost was Marcia," added Ruthie.

Hershel, who probably heard every word of this conversation, reached the bottom of the stairs and pointed at Mr. Zuccini. "Leo," he said. "Am I right?"

"That's Mr. Zuccini, Hershel," said Zoe, "not Leo."

"Oh, Zoe, he means his *sign*," said Ruthie.

"Right!" said Mr. Zuccini, forgetting Hershel's appearance and rushing to him to shake his hand vigorously. "You cast horoscopes? I need one bad! You do one right away for me? I need business possibilities checked." He waved one arm grandly. "Money no object!"

"I'll be glad to do it," said Hershel. "No charge. I need the practice."

Zoe and Ruthie watched as Hershel and Mr. Zuccini walked out of the house, arm in arm, talking like old friends. When they reached the white truck in the driveway, they stood and talked for a few minutes and then they both got in and drove away.

"Boy!" said Ruthie, closing the door. "They sure made friends fast! I never saw Hershel talk so much to a stranger!"

"Hershel and Mr. Zuccini have a lot in common," said Zoe. "Come on, let's do some more cartwheels. We only have two weeks."

After Zoe walked Ruthie as far as the wooded strip that separated the houses on her block from the ones behind them, she fixed herself a peanut butter sandwich and played with the chameleon. He did not, as Ruthie and Mr. Zuccini had said he would, want to stay on her shoulder. He slithered off onto the back of the sofa whenever she sat down, and twice he walked right down her sweater and jeans to the floor, where he was almost impossible to find.

Zoe remembered Ruthie's brother and the string. Rummaging through her mother's sewing box, she found a whole ball of red yarn. She cut off a foot-long piece and tied a neat bow around the chameleon's neck. Pinned to her collar, the lizard had room to run about on her shoulder, but no more. He didn't like the confinement.

When Bob came downstairs to make himself a sandwich, he came into the breakfast room to eat. He eyed the terrarium.

"Where did you get the terrarium and why is there a ball of red yarn in it?" he asked.

"Mr. Zuccini brought me a chameleon. That's his leash."

"His *leash?*"

Zoe got up from the sofa and put down her book. "See? He can go wherever he wants to go, but the ball of yarn stays inside the terrarium. All I have to do to find him is follow the red string."

Bob trailed the yarn from the terrarium to the floor, under the sofa, behind the television set, and up the curtain, where the chameleon flicked out his long tongue at him.

"That's a great idea, Zoe! He surely travels, doesn't he? But are you sure no one will step on him?"

"Not if you keep your eyes open when you see the string."

By midafternoon the chameleon had found the kitchen door and traveled straight across the slippery linoleum to the dining room. The ball of yard grew smaller as it unreeled behind him.

When Zoe went upstairs to work on her room, the hall was crisscrossed with red like a big cat's cradle. She checked to see if there was enough yarn left for a little longer journey.

"Bob, will you watch to see that nobody comes in and steps on him? I have to clean my room."

"O.K. What do I do when the ball of yarn is used up?"

"Call me. I'll come down and wind it up and he can start all over again. Boy, we ought to call him Columbus!"

Zoe was deep in conversation with Ruthie on the upstairs phone when the back door slammed. Her parents were home.

"Got to go, Ruthie. I can't wait to see what Daddy says about the chameleon."

"Wait, just let me tell you one more thing. This absolutely dreamy sixth-grade boy . . ."

When Zoe ran down the stairs and stepped carefully over the yards of yarn in the front hall, she ran into her father in the door of the dining room. He was holding the ball of red yarn from the terrarium and winding it up as he went.

"So there you are! All right, what is it?"

Zoe laughed, since he seemed to be in a good mood. "Keep going, Daddy. You'll find it."

He muttered a little, but the corners of his eyes behind his glasses crinkled a little, as if he might smile, and he kept winding.

He finished the hall and had started through the double doors to the living room, still reeling in red yarn, when Marcia came in.

"Shhhh!" said Zoe, from her perch on the stairway.

Marcia watched her father disappear into the living room. She raised her eyebrows questioningly toward Zoe and peeped through the door.

"Ye gods!" came from the living room.

Zoe jumped up. In the living room, her father was crawling out from under the grand piano, holding the end of the yarn. The chameleon dangled from the full ball.

"I expected at least a Minotaur," he said, disappointed.

"A what?" asked Zoe. "It's a chameleon."

"He means like in the myth, Zoe," Marcia explained. "Don't you know it? Theseus — is it Theseus, Daddy? — goes into the maze after the monster, the Minotaur, and his girl friend shows him how to leave a trail of string, so he can find his way out again."

"I remember now," said Zoe. "I saw it on television. Daddy, you're a pretty good pet namer. I think you'll just have to come up with ideas for all of them. Nice literary names like the Minotaur."

"Ye gods!" said her father, relinquishing the Minotaur

and the ball of yarn. "All the important work I have to do, and you have me finding names."

"Cheer up, Daddy," said Marcia. "Only ten more pets to go."

2

MRS. HANNUM, who was very big on class participation, invited the Minotaur to spend a week in the fifth-grade classroom. She and Zoe arranged a big glass bowl on the nature table for the chameleon, who rode to school in Zoe's blouse pocket.

For the first day, the Minotaur was in some danger of being killed with kindness.

"Just sprinkle a few drops of water on the leaves," Zoe explained to the boy who drew the shortest straw and got to take care of the chameleon for the day. "He won't drink any other way."

When she came back into the room after practice for the gym program, the chameleon's home looked like a miniature rain forest in the monsoon season. Zoe poured the water out into the fountain and decided she'd better put the Minotaur in her pocket, attached to his red leash, whenever she left the room.

She found that food was no problem, when she explained that he loved fresh insects, but added, "except that I'm having a terrible time finding any this time of year."

"We have roaches," said Elmer Evans. "I'll bring some tomorrow."

Tooty, the Edwards's next-door neighbor, turned out to be the best provider, however. The day he was to take care of the Minotaur, he came to school with a jelly jar full of tiny, crawling, winged things.

"They're fruit flies," he explained. "My dad raises them for experiments." Tooty's father taught biology classes at the college where Zoe's father taught literature. He had a room in the basement which he used for a laboratory, which Tooty was rarely allowed into.

"Wow, look at him go!" said Ruthie. The chameleon was in heaven with all the fruit flies to catch. He darted this way and that in the bowl, his long tongue flicking out time after time. The fruit flies didn't have a chance. Finally the Minotaur lay stuffed and sleepy on a rock, and slept.

Tooty watched the hunt carefully. "My dad's got something at home that lizard would love to hunt," he said, "if I can just get one."

Next morning he produced another jelly jar. Inside was one live mosquito, the biggest, nastiest mosquito Zoe had ever seen. Even the Minotaur looked a little doubtful when Tooty slid him under the wire cover of the bowl.

All day the class kept watch to see if the Minotaur could catch this monster of a mosquito. The mosquito hovered and flitted about as much as his enormous size would allow in the bowl, but the Minotaur lay on his rock and tried to look inconspicuous. Occasionally his tongue flicked out tentatively, but he made no attempt to stalk the enemy. When Zoe lifted him out and tied his leash around his neck, he darted in and out of her pocket, obviously relieved to be away from the menacing mosquito.

Mrs. Mills, the principal, dropped in to see the duel.

"My, that's a big mosquito!" she said. "Who brought him?"

Tooty raised his hand proudly. "My dad has lots of them."

Mrs. Mills rattled her keys thoughtfully and peered at the mosquito more closely. "I don't think I ever saw one of those around here," she said as she left the room. "I think I'll look him up."

She was back in the room in ten minutes, frowning and holding a whispered conference at Mrs. Hannum's desk. Then she said, "Terrence?" which nobody ever called Tooty. After glaring the giggling class into silence, she spoke to the red-faced Tooty. "Terrence, where did you say you got that insect?"

"From my father's lab. He does experiments with them. These were a special batch. They came in the mail."

"Does your father know that you brought one to school?"

Well, no, Tooty had to admit that he didn't.

"Well, I'm sorry, but we have to get rid of it. Immediately."

Totally mystified, the class sat in stunned silence as Mrs. Mills wrapped a big handkerchief around her hand, lifted the wire cover of the bowl enough to get her hand inside, and squashed the mosquito. Then she fished out the mosquito, wrapped it in the handkerchief, and dropped both in the wastebasket.

If it had been Mrs. Hannum who did such an unexplainable thing, Zoe would have asked why. But Mrs. Mills was the principal, and fifth-graders don't ask questions of the principal.

Zoe's family was as mystified as she was, when she told them the story at dinner that evening. During dessert the phone rang. Marcia rushed to the kitchen extension and then came back, disgruntled, to say that the call was for Zoe.

It was Tooty. "Hey, Zoe, you know that mosquito?"

"Yes?"

"Well, I told my dad about what happened and he about busted a gut. He said not to tell anybody about the mosquito being at school."

"I won't tell a soul, Tooty. But, why not?"

"He said it's an — wait a minute, he wrote it down — an *Aedes aegypti* mosquito. It came from Panama. I guess it's rare or something."

"Oh! Is that all?"

She went back to the table to explain what Tooty had said. As soon as she said "*Aedes aegypti*," her mother choked on her tea and her father threw back his head and laughed so hard his glasses slid off his hair and fell to the floor behind him.

"What's so funny?" asked Zoe, retrieving the glasses. "I don't get it."

"Yellow fever," Mr. Edwards gasped, wiping his eyes. "I can imagine Tooty's father going before the health board to explain why the whole fifth-grade had yellow fever!"

So the Minotaur went back to fruit flies, which were more his dish, anyway.

Because everyone who wanted to had not had his chance to take care of the chameleon for a day, Zoe kept him at school for another week. But she continued to pin him, red leash and all, inside her pocket whenever she had to go up to the auditorium to practice for the gym class's assembly program. Since she had been wearing her shorts to school under her skirt, to save running downstairs to the locker room and then back up to the auditorium for practice, she always wore a blouse and had a pocket to put him in. When she and Ruthie did their cartwheels, she gave the Minotaur to Mr. NcNulty to hold.

On the morning of the program, Zoe was as nervous as Ruthie had been all along. Whirling head over heels around an empty stage, or on your own front porch, was much easier than doing it in front of an auditorium full of yelling, cat-calling, booing, cheering sixth-graders.

The noise during most of the acts was deafening. Zoe and Ruthie stood in the wings during the human pyramid, listening. Peeping out front, Zoe saw Mrs. Mills stand up from her seat in the front row and glare at everybody, which quieted them for only a few minutes.

"I don't think I can do it," Zoe whispered to Ruthie, who stood beside her waiting her turn at the peephole and chewing gum busily.

"Easy," said Ruthie. "Just act like you're at home. Hurry up, Zoe. I want to get another look at all those boys."

Zoe was helping Ruthie peel bubble gum off the curtain below the peephole when Mr. McNulty tiptoed up in his gym shoes.

"All right, girls. You're next. Give us a big finish now! Remember, three times around, stop in front of the stage and bow, and move back so the curtain can close. Move aside now! Here come the tumblers."

The sweating, exhausted boys stumbled past them and Zoe and Ruthie raised their arms, turned sideways, and cartwheeled out onto the stage.

Zoe went in front, to set the pace. She was so busy she barely heard the yelling and whistling and clapping out front. And all she could see was a kaleidoscopic blur of gray curtain at the back of the stage changing into confetti colors as they whirled past the audience.

But suddenly, dangling right in front of her nose where she couldn't help but see it, was a red string.

The chameleon was not on it.

She stopped so suddenly she fell, and Ruthie crashed into her. They lay tangled at the front of the stage. Zoe eased herself up on her elbows, but Ruthie didn't move.

The whistling and cheering had stopped abruptly. There was a loud collective gasp, and the audience began to murmur. Here and there people stood up to see what was happening on stage.

Zoe groped about on the floor, unaware of the audience's reaction. Mr. McNulty came bounding out on stage, blowing his whistle and yelling, "Don't move! Broken bones . . ."

"STOP!" screamed Zoe. Mr. McNulty stopped.

Mrs. Mills started toward the stairway leading to stage left. She had one foot poised on the top step when Zoe yelled "STOP!" at her. The principal froze with one foot still in the air.

The murmur in the audience grew louder. More people stood up, possibly wondering about Zoe's strange power over the faculty. Zoe went on crawling about the stage, feeling every inch of the floor around Ruthie's motionless body.

"Zoe!" she heard someone say, from almost beside her. Mrs. Hannum stood in front of the stage, but on the floor where the audience was. She had not risked coming up the steps as Mrs. Mills and Mr. McNulty, still frozen where Zoe had stopped them, had done. She leaned her arms on the stage floor, her head reaching just above the level of the stage, and said, "What is it? What's wrong?"

"Mrs. Hannum, I've lost the Minotaur."

Mrs. Hannum's face was a picture of relief. She almost laughed. "Well, slide over here and get off. We'll find him, but you can't ruin Mr. McNulty's program! Come on now, slide. Ruthie, you too. Ruthie? *Ruthie?*"

Ruthie sat up, slowly, and turned her head from side to side. "What happened?" she asked. "Where am I?"

"Never mind that, Ruthie. Slide over here. Off the stage. Mr. McNulty," she called, "close the curtain. Keep everybody off-stage."

The curtain closed immediately, nearly knocking over the gym teacher, who was as puzzled as everyone else in the auditorium. After the bewildered sixth-graders had filed out, the class searched the stage.

At lunchtime the hunt was called off. Zoe couldn't eat her lunch for worrying about the chameleon, but Ruthie ate for both of them, glorying in all the attention and enjoying the sling on her bruised arm.

After school they went back to the auditorium. "He could be anywhere," said Zoe, looking at the yards and yards of curtains. "We'll never find him. How am I going to tell Mr. Zuccini I lost my pet?"

Mrs. Mills let her put a sign on the auditorium doors reading CAUTION! CHAMELEON LOOSE. REWARD FOR CAPTURE. But no one claimed the reward.

ARIES

●

March 21 – April 20

Zoe walked stiffly home from her piano lesson, balancing her Czerny exercise book on her head. She took her time, enjoying the warm evening and trying to be too late to set the table for dinner. Two weeks ago, she remembered, she had had to run to get home before dark. Now the streetlights hadn't even been turned on.

She stooped down to admire a crocus on a lawn and jumped when a horn blew sharply behind her. Looking around, she didn't recognize the strange red truck, but Mr. Zuccini was behind the wheel. He looked worried.

"Get in, Zoe! Quick!"

She had time to notice that the black medallions

painted all over the red truck were zodiac signs as she ran around and climbed in. "You painted your truck, Mr. Zuccini. It looks great!"

"You like?" He put the truck in gear and roared away. "Hershel's idea. He's a good man for publicity. And horoscopes. I keep him."

The truck sped past the Edwards house, picked up speed, and rounded a corner.

"Where are we going?" asked Zoe. "I have to tell my — "

"I told her already. I was there waiting for you. Finally went to get you at piano lesson, but you had left." He turned his head and winked at Zoe. "Nice lady you got for piano teacher!"

Zoe wrinkled her nose. "Mrs. Petrovich?"

"She — *married* lady?"

"I think she's a widow. Mr. Zuccini, where are we going?"

"You see when we get there. Got to hurry." He went through a yellow light, turned a corner, and sped across the campus bridge.

"What did you mean, you kept Hershel? Do you mean you gave him a job?"

He nodded. "After school. On weekends. Hershel is good worker. Adds atmosphere."

Zoe suddenly noticed what Mr. Zuccini was wearing. "Why, you've got a cape just like Hershel's."

"You like?" he asked with a broad grin. He shifted in his seat so that Zoe could see the zodiac sign on the back. "Hershel's idea, too. I have lion. Hershel has ram. He's Aries."

The truck screeched to a halt before a small white building. Zoe had to run to keep up with Mr. Zuccini, heavy as he was. "Why are we in such a hurry?" she asked, taking the steps two at a time. "Where are we?"

"A.S.P.C.A. Got to rescue a dog."

"*Rescue a dog?*"

"Got to get him before closing. Hurry." He rushed through a reception room where a typist was covering her typewriter and into a small, white room beyond. It looked like a doctor's examining room, Zoe thought. Somewhere she could hear dogs barking and one howling cat.

Chained to a table leg in the room they were in was just one dog.

He was a fat, grizzled old bulldog, grayish white. He was sound asleep on the floor, his hind legs splayed out behind him. He had purple feet.

"You like?" Mr. Zuccini looked from Zoe to the dog anxiously.

"Well — what's the matter with his feet?"

"Medicine. Bites his nails. He is very old, very nervous. No one wants him. Been here as long as they can keep him. Going to put him to sleep if no one claims him by closing time. I meant to give you puppy later, Zoe, when your papa used to pets. But — " He spread his arm toward the old dog, who opened one eye, sighed until his jowls quivered, and went back to sleep.

"Put him to sleep! You mean — *forever?*" Zoe had a fleeting vision of her father's face when he saw the dog. The vision dissolved into one of the bulldog being dragged, asleep and innocent, into the gas chamber. "Oh, no! Get him into the truck, quick!"

Mr. Zuccini lifted her right off her feet with his hug.

Zoe half led, half dragged what must have been sixty-five pounds of dead weight out the door while Mr. Zuccini signed some papers. While she paused outside to catch her breath and notice that darkness had come while they were inside, the dog went to sleep on the steps. Mr. Zuccini picked him up and laid him gently in the truck. Zoe rode in back with him, chewing the end of her braid and rubbing the dog's heavy head. For a while they rode silently through the dark streets.

Then Mr. Zuccini half turned his head to ask, "Zoe? What your father going to say?"

Zoe looked down at the dark muzzle in her lap and answered, with more assurance than she felt, "Don't worry. When he sees this beautiful dog he won't be able to say a word."

Mr. Edwards was speechless for about thirty seconds, however, when Zoe yelled from the hall for everybody to come quick. The bulldog lay beside her on the rug in front of the door, exhausted and asleep. Mr. Zuccini had deposited him there and then roared away in the red truck, grinning apologetically. Coward, thought Zoe, as she waited for her father to appear at the study door. She could hear her mother and Bob and Marcia coming through the dining room.

Mr. Edwards came out of his study, saw the dog, and stopped to pull his glasses down for a better look. Zoe took a deep breath and waited.

"Ye gods! Get that monster out of here!"

"Oh, look at the dog!" Marcia ran to him when she saw him.

"Out!"

Bob laughed when he came through the hall. "Look at that! He's so homely he's beautiful!"

The bulldog opened one eye and raised his head long

enough to drool on the rug. Marcia rubbed his ears gently. He sighed and closed his eye.

"Out!" Mr. Edwards waved both arms wildly toward the door.

"Poor thing," said Mrs. Edwards, coming to bend over him. "What's wrong with his feet?"

"Out!"

"A watchdog isn't a bad idea, Dad," said Bob. Zoe thought this dog probably couldn't stay awake long enough to watch anything, but she didn't say so.

"Out!" Mr. Edwards waved his arms again.

"He can sleep in the basement, dear," said Mrs. Edwards.

"I'll build him a house," said Bob.

"Out!" The voice was desperate.

Marcia scratched the dog's drooping jowls. "Oh, Daddy, he won't be any trouble, will you, doggie?"

The dog opened his eyes, raised his head, and grinned. His tongue lolled out. Quite definitely, he seemed to like Marcia.

"Out!" said Mr. Edwards, a little less loudly.

"Daddy, I've practiced every day! My room is spotless!"

"Out! I was given veto power and I'm using it. Out!"

Zoe sighed, looked wide-eyed at the dog's colored feet, and thought of the lepers marooned on some island in Hawaii. A tear splashed down her nose.

"Out!" The arms waved rather vaguely, then fell to his sides.

"Come on, old dog," said Zoe sadly, tugging on his chain. "It's the gas chamber for you in the morning."

Mr. Edwards opened his mouth and formed an O, but

nothing came out. He glared at Zoe, who sniffed loudly, and then at the rest of his family in turn. "You are all against me," he said grumpily. "My word means nothing here."

Marcia went to him and put her arm around his shoulders. "Daddy," she said solemnly, "we love you too much to keep this poor, homeless, sad old dog if you say not to. You just say the word and we'll send him away to be slaughtered."

Mr. Edwards's face sagged in defeat. He walked slowly back toward the study, his shoulders bent. At the door he turned.

"You'll all be sorry for this," he said. "Taking advantage of an old man."

"Daddy, you're a pussy cat!"

"I am *not* a pussy cat," he said severely, fighting off Marcia's kisses, "but a misunderstood, persecuted, softhearted old fool. Now get that monster into the basement. He's drooling all over the rug."

Zoe made the dog a bed on an old blanket in the laundry room, where he seemed content to sleep around the clock. The only thing he liked better than a good nap was a good meal. And he liked Marcia. Zoe couldn't understand it. Marcia condescended to feed him only once, and she gave up taking him for an evening walk when she found it was more an evening drag. But when Mr. Edwards was out of the house and Zoe brought the dog upstairs, he went straight to Marcia and slept with his grizzled head on her foot.

"Maybe it's because she smells good," said Bob, watching the dog snooze.

"I don't smell bad!" said Zoe indignantly. "Do I?"

Bob laughed. "Of course not — but you don't use Chanel, either."

Marcia moved cautiously, so she wouldn't disturb the dog, and held up a book. "I just found a nice doggie quote," she said. "Listen to this: 'If you pick up a starving dog and make him prosperous, he won't bite you. This is the main difference between a dog and a man.'"

Zoe thought about it. "That's not true. If you help somebody, they'll help you when you need it."

Marcia laughed. "Zoe, you're too innocent. You'll learn better."

"What is the quotation from, Marcia?" asked Bob.

"Mark Twain. It's in a book I have to read for a book report. *Pudd'nhead Wilson*."

"There's a good literary name for the dog," said Bob, looking up from a drawing he was making at the desk. "That dog is a Pudd'nhead if I ever saw one."

Zoe frowned. "It's too — undignified. I was thinking about either Lad or White Fang."

Bob got up from the desk, laughing as he rolled up his sketch, and crossed the room to the kitchen door. "That dog hasn't been a lad in years, Zoe. And as for White Fang — he's hardly got a tooth in his head." He held up the roll of paper. "I'm going out to the workshop and start Pudd'nhead's house, by the way."

Zoe jumped up. "Can I come?"

"No! You can't see the house until June fourteenth — if it's finished."

"That's my birthday. And it's *months* away!"

"It may not be long enough away for what I have in mind," Bob said mysteriously, as he opened the kitchen door. "There's Dad's car pulling in the garage," he called back. "Better get Pudd'nhead in the basement."

Zoe, with Marcia's help, shoved the dog through the kitchen and down the basement steps. Zoe stayed downstairs to do her homework on the ironing board, where she could keep the dog company. He didn't seem to mind listening to the multiplication tables, and he was usually asleep before she finished the threes.

Zoe had just finished clearing off three spoons, a saucer, and two glasses from her working space when Marcia called down the steps, "I have to get ready to go out, Zoe. Will you let Roger in when he comes, so Daddy won't scare him to death?"

Zoe didn't particularly want to talk to Roger either, but she yelled back, "O.K.," since Marcia had been pretty nice lately.

But when the bell sounded faintly from upstairs and she ran up to answer the door, her father was already ushering Roger in. Zoe knew he must have been passing through the hall when the bell rang, because her father never answered a ringing phone or doorbell when there was anyone else to do it.

Zoe peeped through the dining-room door. Roger didn't look too bad, if you liked crew cuts and narrow ties, she thought. She heard her father say, not very enthusiastically, "Will you come into the study and wait? Marcia shouldn't be long."

"Thank you, sir," said Roger pleasantly, and followed Mr. Edwards into the room.

Zoe tiptoed to the study door and found she could see her father in his wicker rocking chair when she looked through the slot between the door and its frame. She had to cover her mouth to keep from giggling at her father's sour face. She moved a few inches and was able to see Roger, who was shoving aside a stack of papers to make room on the sofa.

After they agreed that it was a nice evening, Roger and Mr. Edwards didn't seem to agree on anything else.

"Interesting chair you have there," Roger said.

"Very comfortable," said Mr. Edwards.

"Of course I prefer a modern recliner," said Roger.

"Oh?" Mr. Edwards picked up his newspaper from the floor.

"Anything good on the market today?" Roger asked.

"Market? Market?" Mr. Edwards ruffled through the food section.

"Stock market. My father and I always check out our stocks."

"Oh. Oh, I wouldn't know about the market. I was reading the editorial page."

"I think that paper has excellent editorials, don't you?" asked Roger. "My father says they are good, solid, conservative opinion."

Zoe leaned against the wall outside the door and held both hands over her mouth.

Mr. Edwards's silence apparently made Roger a little uncomfortable, and he shifted a little on the sofa. He tried again. "Perhaps you know my father, sir? He's president of Wilson Construction Company."

"That the firm that's trying to tear down the old houses across the campus for a shopping center?"

"That's the one," said Roger proudly. "Time for progress, my father says."

"Excuse me a minute," said Mr. Edwards. He came out of the room so suddenly that he caught Zoe trying to look casual outside. "Tell your sister," he hissed, "that I'll give her five seconds to get down here."

Zoe heard him muttering as he stalked into the living room with his newspaper.

TAURUS

April 21 – May 22

1

Zoe's mother rushed her family through dinner so she could get to the PTA meeting on schedule.

"Bring me something good," yelled Zoe from the basement. They always had refreshments left over.

"Must that child take her meals in the cellar?" asked Mr. Edwards. "It's bad enough that she studies down there."

"It's only dessert, dear," said Mrs. Edwards, putting on her coat in the kitchen. "And it does keep her room cleaner."

"Except now we have to go downstairs when we need spoons instead of up," said Marcia. "Did she ever find the asparagus tongs? We're going to need them when Roger comes to dinner."

"Fresh asparagus," said Mrs. Edwards, opening the door to go out to the garage, "is not on the menu. And we are *not* eating in the dining room."

"But Roger's family always — " She broke off as the door slammed.

Zoe was climbing into bed with her multiplication flash cards when her mother came in. She still had her coat on, and she was carrying a white box from the bakery.

"Yummy!" said Zoe, and opened the lid.

The Minotaur flicked out his tongue at a brownie crumb and looked up at her.

"How — where — " Zoe stammered.

Mrs. Edwards sat down on the edge of the bed and unbuttoned her coat. "I wish your father had seen it," she began. "He'd never again talk about how dull PTA meetings are. Well, actually, it was pretty dull at first. I was just dozing off during the reading of the minutes, when the secretary screamed. *Loudly.* Into the mike. Everybody in the auditorium jumped, and a lady in the front row fainted. They had to carry her out."

"The secretary saw — "

"The Minotaur!" Mrs. Edwards giggled, remembering. "Apparently he was sitting on top of the microphone making faces at her."

"Oh, no!"

"Oh, yes. Of course we didn't know what had made her scream. All we could see was Mrs. Mills getting up, picking something off the mike, and patting the secretary on the shoulder. Then she sat down and put something in her purse, and the meeting calmed down. We didn't find out what it was all about until refreshment time."

"I'm glad he's home," said Zoe. "This is better than a cupcake any day."

On Saturday Zoe and Ruthie took the Minotaur for a walk. They lay on the slope at the very back of the long lawn, where the woods separating the Edwards's property from the next block began, and watched the chameleon bask in the sun. The red leash moved only a little as he explored the jumble of rocks where Mrs. Edwards made a garden in the summer.

Zoe had just turned over on her back to watch the clouds when a familiar voice called from the driveway in front of the garage, and a horn blew. She sat up quickly and saw two black cloaks getting out of a red truck.

"Hi, Mr. Zuccini! Hi, Hershel! Come on back and see the chameleon!"

As the thin figure and the fat one strolled across the lawn toward them, Ruthie said, "If Hershel doesn't get a haircut, his hair is going to be as long as yours, Zoe."

"Hardly," asid Zoe. "I can sit on mine. It's *never* been cut. So Hershel's got about nine years to go." She picked up the end of her braid absently and watched Mr. Zuccini stop in the middle of the lawn to look at the house.

"Oh-oh," said Ruthie. "He's going to offer to buy your house again."

"He loves this place," said Zoe. "He should have a house and a family."

"Listen to you! And you're always talking about *me* matchmaking!"

Zoe jumped up as Mr. Zuccini began to climb the gen-

tle slope where she and Ruthie had lain. He inspected
the chameleon carefully and pronounced him healthy.
"Must have plenty bugs in your school, Zoe. But how did
he get water?"

"Mrs. Hannum thought he must have found a pipe with
moisture condensed on it."

"Ah! Of course. Well, he's in good shape." Mr. Zuc-

cini spread his cape and sat down on the slope to enjoy
the spring sunshine. "Wonderful house you have here,
Zoe! And yard! Your mother the gardener?"

Zoe nodded. "We're sitting right by the rock garden.
Of course it doesn't look like much. But in summer it's
pretty."

Hershel inspected the remains of a crumbling rock wall
that extended partly around the rocks. "Didn't this used
to be a pool?"

"I think it was a fishpond when the house was new,"
Zoe answered. "When Bob filled in the hole for Mother
he found a fish skeleton."

"Fishpond," said Mr. Zuccini. "Ah, those were the days!
Why not make it a pond again?"

"Mother would love it, but Daddy started yelling about
bulldozers and bills, so we never did."

"Hershel," Ruthie interrupted, "you never did my horo-
scope."

"There wasn't a boy in it," Hershel answered. "I thought
you'd be too disappointed. Anyway, I've given up astrology."

"What are you doing now?" Ruthie eyed his cloak and
took a guess. "Magic?"

Hershel leaned over and poked a twig through her
bubble. "Nope. ESP."

"Hershel trying to communicate with the dead," said
Mr. Zuccini. "Spent all morning in shop talking to Mozart."

"Oh, is he dead?" asked Ruthie.

Hershel groaned and got up. Dusting off his cloak he
conversation? Such appalling ignorance!"
said, "Let's go, Mr. Zuccini. How can we hold a civilized

Mr. Zuccini heaved his bulk off the grass with some difficulty and stopped Zoe as she got up, too. "No, no! We came to see something very interesting in garage workshop. You *not* allowed."

"Can I go?" asked Ruthie. "I'm dying to see that doghouse."

"Ruthie Bishop, you sit right down," said Zoe. "If I can't see it, you can't."

Mr. Zuccini stopped by the jumble of rocks and the fragment of wall for a moment and looked at it closely. "Fishpond, eh?" he said, and then walked back across the lawn with Hershel.

Three days later he came back, put more purple medicine on Pudd'nhead's feet, offered to buy the house, praised Mrs. Edwards's doughnuts, and left an incubator.

"An incubator! What do you mean, an incubator?"

"You know, Daddy — to hatch things."

"And what and where is this incubator hatching things?" Mr. Edwards looked under his chair as if he expected to find an egg there.

"In my room. Come and see."

Marcia and Bob joined the parade up the stairs, Marcia giggling and Bob shushing her.

In Zoe's dark bedroom, sitting at the foot of her bed, was a square metal box. The electric bulb inside cast round pools of light on the blue rug through the peepholes on each side. Mr. Edwards got down on his hands and knees to look through one of the holes at the single egg inside, sitting solitary and mysterious.

"Ye gods," he muttered as he got to his feet.

"Daddy, don't get difficult now," said Marcia. "Think

how educational this is for Zoe. The miracle of birth and all that."

"It's not the hatching I'm objecting to," Mr. Edwards said. "It's the hatchee. I don't want the tenant of any egg living in my house."

"It can live in the back yard," said Bob, kicking a spoon under the bed. "Just look at this room. Spotless!"

"Well, we'll see, but I can tell you it will have to go after a while," Mr. Edwards said. He turned at the doorway. "Probably won't even hatch. It's cracked, you know."

"Cracked!"

All three of them dived for a peephole.

"It's hatching!"

"Bring hot water!"

"Oh, Bob, not for an *egg!*"

It took hours for the damp, feeble little creature to peck its way out of the shell. Mrs. Edwards dragged them away at intervals for homework, chores, piano practice.

"Honestly, Mother, I'll bet you'll drag me out of the hospital when I'm having a baby if my name is on the schedule to do dishes," grumbled Marcia as she rushed downstairs to dry the plates.

"I know exactly how an expectant father feels," groaned Bob, dropping on the sofa in the breakfast room late in the evening.

"I know," said Marcia, accepting a cup of tea from her mother. "I'm exhausted."

"I don't know how you could be," her mother said calmly. "All you did was dry two forks and complain."

Zoe tiptoed in, giggling. "Everybody stay here," she

said, looking behind her. "Daddy just sneaked up the stairs for a look while we're out of the bedroom."

Marcia hooted. "Let's go tease him!"

Mrs. Edwards shook her head. "I don't think that's wise," she said. "Your father has his image to protect."

"Does it always take this long?" asked Bob. "Can't we help it out of its shell?"

"You have to let it do the work itself," Zoe said, sipping her tea. "That's the way it gets strong enough to face the world."

Zoe fell asleep on the rug, watching the new arrival complete his journey into the world. Her mother had to shake her to get her up.

"Zoe, it's midnight! You'll never get up for school."

"I wanted to see it when it got out," Zoe answered. "Mother, I think I know why Mr. Zuccini was so interested in the fishpond the other day. Can we build it again?"

"Whatever made you think of that now?"

"Look in the incubator."

Mrs. Edwards gathered her robe around her knees and stooped down to a peephole. "Good heavens, it's a *duck!* Whatever is your father going to say?"

"Ye gods," said Zoe sleepily.

2

ZOE STAMPED UP the front steps, slammed the door, stormed into the living room, and flung her music in the general direction of the piano.

"This is absolutely the last year I am taking piano lessons!" she announced. "Mother, how *could* you?"

"How could I what, dear?" Mrs. Edwards asked mildly, looking up from the dress pattern she was pinning on the blue material spread on the rug. "Pick up your music."

"Mrs. Petrovich informed me, absolutely *raving* about how nice you are, that we're having the recital *here!*"

"Why, yes, she asked for a volunteer because her house is so crowded with the pianos and the harpsichord and the organ. It's all right, Zoe. I checked the schedule."

"Well, I wish you'd checked with me!" Zoe flipped up her braid and sat down hard on the sofa. "I'm absolutely humiliated!"

"What's the difference?" asked Marcia, handing pins to her mother. "You have to play whether it's here or there."

"I know, but everybody will think I *like* it!"

"Well, you're silly not to," Marcia said. "I wish Mother and Daddy had made *me* go on with piano. Sylvia Barnes plays so well she got asked to play with a group."

"I don't want to play with any old group," said Zoe grumpily.

"With a disposition like that nobody will ever ask you, so don't worry," snapped Marcia.

"That's enough, both of you," said Mrs. Edwards.

"The recital *here*," Zoe muttered, lashing at her own knee with her braid. "You just wait until this summer. No more music lessons! No more practicing! I'm never going to look at another piece of music!"

Mrs. Edwards took some pins from her mouth and looked around at Zoe. "It seems to me," she said quietly, "that some time ago, when you wanted something very

much, you made a few promises about accepting a little
more responsibility. And I seem to remember that practicing the piano was one of the promises. Even Mr. Zuccini insisted on that. Or have you forgotten?"

Zoe squirmed a little. "Well, no, I haven't forgotten.
But do you mean I have to practice in the *summer?*"

"It was your promise, dear."

"But that's not fair!" wailed Zoe, beginning to chew her
braid.

Mrs. Edwards's eyebrows raised as far as they would
go. "Pick up that music, Zoe. And while you're doing it,
you might think about the clothes and books and cracker
crumbs and *spoons* strewn all over your room. I seem to
recall a promise about that, too. Or isn't that *fair?*"

Mrs. Edwards rarely used sarcasm with her children.
When she did, Zoe thought as she meekly picked up the
scattered sheets of music, she could make you feel about
half as tall as the Minotaur.

"I'll clean it after dinner," she told her mother. "And
say the multiplication tables, too."

"I should think so," Mrs. Edwards answered. "From
the looks of the last arithmetic papers, you couldn't have
been working very hard. Of course, if you don't think it's
fair —"

"It's fair," said Zoe. "I'm sorry."

Marcia giggled suddenly. "Oh, I'm not laughing at you,
Zoe! I can't wait to see Daddy's face when he finds out
we're going to have twenty-five kids and about a hundred
parents here for a recital."

"Oh, he won't care. He's the music lover, after all,"
said Mrs. Edwards breezily. She sat back on her heels and
looked around the long room, from the small grand piano

at one end to the double doors leading to the front hall at the other end. "Anyway, it's already on the schedule."

"Where are we going to put everybody?" asked Zoe.

"We'll put folding chairs facing the piano, of course, with an aisle in the center of the room." Mrs. Edwards pointed to the French doors, open to the porch. "And we'll put the picnic benches out there for the students. When it's someone's turn to play, he can come right through the doors to the piano. Keeps the squirmers happy, too. And of course for refreshments — "

"Refreshments!" said Zoe. "Why does it have to be such a production?"

"Mrs. Petrovich will handle all that," answered Mrs. Edwards. "Of course there's the cleaning — "

"Cleaning!" wailed Marcia. "Nobody's going to know if the house is dirty!"

"I know," said Mrs. Edwards. "But it's a good chance to get the spring cleaning on the schedule. Marcia, you'd better check the roast. And Zoe, Mr. Zuccini called. He says Hans can have his first swim any time." She reached for the pinking shears. "If you'll fill the laundry tub, we'll put him in after dinner."

The recital forgotten, and far in the future anyway, Zoe ran downstairs to fill the tub.

Hans, named after the creator of the Ugly Duckling, snuggled into Zoe's cupped hands as she lifted him from his box by Pudd'nhead's bed. The whole family gathered around the plastic laundry tub to watch his first swimming lesson — even Mr. Edwards, who looked around the laundry room curiously.

"I don't think I've ever been in this room," he commented. "Certainly is a strange home for a duck."

"Yes, you have," said Mrs. Edwards dryly. "Three years ago when Bob broke his ankle and you had to come down here looking for the snow shovel."

"Ruthie's brother got an Easter duck once," said Zoe. "It lived in their basement for a year."

"Ye gods!"

"What happened to it?" asked Marcia. "No, wait, don't tell me. I don't think I want to know."

"They took it to the pond on the campus where the flock of ducks is," Zoe told her, and then shut her mouth quickly as she realized her father had heard.

"Come on, Zoe. Put him in," said Bob.

Zoe cradled the warm, fragile body in her hands over the water. The duck fluttered his downy, incredibly delicate wings, and quacked. "In you go, Hans. Sink or swim."

He sank, immediately, like a badly weighted bathtub toy. And then he came up, quacking, quivering, working his tiny orange feet furiously. He turned a somersault, rose, shook water on Mr. Edwards, and sailed around the outer edge of the red plastic tub as if he had been swimming for months.

"Amazing," said Mr. Edwards, pulling down his glasses to inspect the duck's scissoring feet.

"Isn't he getting beautiful?" asked Zoe. "I wish we had a picture of him."

"Well, you'd better get it right away," answered her father, "because he's going to outgrow that tub in no time. And then what?"

Zoe looked at her mother and asked, "Is this a good time? He may not be in a better mood for a week."

"We thought," said Mrs. Edwards, "that we might fix

up the old fishpond for the duck. Bob says it wouldn't take much — "

"What!" The glasses went up on the forehead again. "All that for a *duck!* Don't be ridiculous. Think of the expense, the inconvenience, the earth-moving equipment. I haven't time for all that. I have Important Work to do!"

"I'll do it, Dad," said Bob. "It won't be bad at all. The stones are there, you know. It's a pick-and-shovel-and-garden-hose job."

Since Bob had said it, Mr. Edwards considered it. But he shook his head. "No. It's out of the question. Now I've got to get to work."

He stumbled over Pudd'nhead, who had staggered out of his bed to the tub. The dog hung his head over the edge, lapped a few mouthfuls, and went to sleep with his muzzle in the water. The duck paddled over.

"That's the longest distance I've see that monster walk since he invaded," said Mr. Edwards.

"I walk him twice a day!" said Zoe indignantly.

"That's *walking?*" asked Marcia sarcastically. "The only time he really walks is from his bed to his dinner."

"And speaking of dinner," said Mr. Edwards, "how much does that monster eat, anyway? The pantry looks like the assembly line of the Gaines factory."

"We buy in quantity to save money," said Mrs. Edwards. "And it all comes out of Zoe's allowance. I made up a payment schedule."

"I'm glad to feed a starving dog," said Zoe firmly. "He won't bite me, which is more than I can say for some of the people here!"

"Ye gods!" said Mr. Edwards, turning to leave the room.

"She's learning," said Marcia to Bob.

From the top of the steps, Mr. Edwards shouted down, "Remember, the day that duck outgrows that tub is the day he goes! I'm exercising my veto power, such as it is. I will *not* have a poultry farm in my cellar!"

The door slammed. Zoe looked at her mother desperately. Mrs. Edwards trailed a finger in the water and watched the duck for a moment.

Finally she stood up. "Bob, are you sure the job isn't too much for you?"

"No. I can do it. But it'll take a little time. I still haven't finished the you-know-what in the shop. And Saturday the schedule says to hose off the back porch and get the summer furniture out, so that day is gone."

Mrs. Edwards nodded. "All right. Let's do it. But we'll have to keep it a secret. You'll have to work when your father is either busy in the study or at the college."

Bob grinned. "O.K. But who gets blamed for it if he catches us?"

"Me," said Zoe. "I'll tell him I talked you into it."

"No, no," said Mrs. Edwards. "This is my responsibility. We'll just have to think of something to make him think it was his own idea."

On Saturday Zoe helped Bob bring the summer furniture for the screened porch from the garage. She hosed off the floor and helped him lay the fiber rug over the concrete. Then they spread newspapers in the yard to protect the new grass while Bob painted.

Zoe did the top of the porch table while Bob lay on his back and painted the underside and the legs. When Marcia yelled "Zoe!" at the top of her lungs from inside the house, Zoe was so startled that she almost painted her braid.

"What did you do now?" Bob asked from under the table.

"I don't know," said Zoe, listening to Marcia yell her name all the way through the house, "but she sure is mad."

"Keep still and maybe you can avoid her until she cools off."

"There you are, you little brat!" said Marcia as she came from the kitchen to the porch. She slammed the porch door behind her, crossed the few feet of lawn to where Zoe stood, paintbrush in hand, and stood with her hands on her hips. Her face was almost ugly because of her anger.

Under the table, Bob continued to paint with even strokes. "No need to get nasty," he said mildly.

"I'm going to tell Daddy about that duck just as soon as he gets back!" said Marcia, paying no attention to Bob.

"But what did he *do*?" asked Zoe.

"I was never so embarrassed in my life!" Marcia went on. "Roger came up on the porch with me, and there was this duck swimming around in that red tub! And this — this *pen* made out of window screens propped against the banister. I was simply humiliated!"

"He's not hurting anything out there," said Zoe. "The banisters make a good cage and he has to have some fresh air. He's just too big for his box, Marcia!"

"Our house looks like a *slum!*"

"What did Roger say?" asked Bob.

"Oh, he didn't *say* anything! But can you imagine a duck on the Wilsons' porch? They don't even have a porch — it's a *terrace!*"

Bob put his brush down on a newspaper and stood up

so he could look down at her. "Maybe you could bring Roger around to the back door," he said slowly, "or isn't the servants' entrance good enough for *you?*"

Marcia turned on her heel and ran into the house. They could hear her slamming doors all the way upstairs.

Zoe stood miserably by the half-painted table, but Bob crawled back underneath and went on painting calmly.

"We just *have* to get the pond fixed," said Zoe.

"We will. Forget Marcia," Bob said. "Put Hans in the workshop — tub and all. And do it now, before she gets to Dad."

Apparently Roger survived the shock of discovering a duck on his girl's porch, because he came to pick her up Saturday evening, as usual.

Zoe, Ruthie, Pudd'nhead, and Hans let him step over their various arms and legs, wings and tails as he went up the front steps.

"Hello, girls," he said, pleasantly enough.

Zoe glared at him. "Want to pet my dog?" she challenged him.

"Nice dog," Roger said, patting the wrinkled forehead gingerly.

"Careful," said Ruthie. "He's vicious, especially to people who wear too much aftershave lotion."

Roger took his hand away quickly.

"Want to hold my duck?" Zoe asked him wickedly.

"No — no, thanks. We've met." Roger began easing sideways up the steps.

"Want to see her cricket?" Ruthie asked before he could get away.

"Want to wear my chameleon?" Zoe asked.

"Want to feed the seal?" said Ruthie innocently.

"Seal?" Roger looked as if he believed it. "How many pets do you have, anyway? Marcia didn't say any-thing — "

"Oh, just a few more," Ruthie told him, counting on her fingers. "There's the alligator, and — "

"*Alligator?*"

"And the king snake and the baby buffalo and the os-trich — "

"*Ostrich?*"

"And don't forget the dragon and the new centaur," Zoe added.

And they jumped up, grabbed the duck, and ran around the house giggling.

GEMINI

May 23 – June 21

MR. Edwards was fond of quoting to Zoe that it was
better to have a little music, however bad, singing madly
in the soul than none at all. But as time for the recital approached, he grew curiously silent on the subject. In fact,
he fled the house as often as he could.

One reason for his desertion of the study was the flurry
of housecleaning that went on for two weeks before the
recital. Mrs. Edwards did the house from top to bottom.
Something was always going out or coming back — rugs,
drapes, slipcovers — and someone was always scouring,
dusting, vacuuming.

"*Why* do I have to do my room?" asked Zoe. "It's so

clean now it almost squeaks! And nobody from the recital
is going to be up *there!*"

"You never know," said Mrs. Edwards. "Anyway, it's on
the schedule."

Marcia giggled and was promptly sent to wash woodwork in the living room, where she complained all morning.

"What if Roger were to come in?" she moaned. "I don't
know why we can't have a charwoman."

Mrs. Edwards's eyebrows went up. "In the United
States we call them cleaning ladies," she said. "And in this
house, especially. Charwoman, indeed! Be sure you get
the dust above the doors."

Mr. Edwards saw Marcia blocking the doorway, dust-
cap on her curls, Zoe shining the banister and blocking
the stairs, and Mrs. Edwards dusting the pictures by
the study door, blocking that exit. He fled to the campus
again, and Bob went straight to the back yard to deepen
the hole he had begun.

Another reason for Mr. Edwards's flights was that many
of the children in the recital began having their lessons or
at least a practice at the Edwards's piano, so they could
get accustomed to the action of a strange instrument.
Since few of the older students or teen-agers could be in-
duced to come, Mr. Edwards was apparently forced to
conclude that all of Mrs. Petrovich's pupils were totally un-
talented.

"Ye gods!" he exclaimed as he listened to some small
wretch struggle through "The Stars and Stripes Forever."
"That child should be forbidden ever to touch a musical
instrument."

And he grabbed his briefcase and drove off to the

campus for a little peace and quiet. Mrs. Edwards, with a shout of triumph, entered the study, broom and mop in hand.

The day before the recital Ruthie and Zoe practiced their pieces and then relaxed with the dog, the chameleon, and the cricket on the back porch. Pudd'nhead had discovered the glider at the end of the porch near the driveway and exerted himself enough to climb onto it. He had to be dragged away bodily at night.

"Doesn't your father yell about him always being there?" asked Ruthie, watching Pudd'nhead snooze with his head hanging over the edge of a cushion.

Zoe rocked the glider gently. "As long as he's not in Daddy's chaise longue, he's allowed," she said. "As a matter of fact, you'd better get out of it before he comes home."

"With pleasure," said Ruthie, squirming off the end of the long chair. "This is the lumpiest thing I ever sat on."

"I know," said Zoe. "But Daddy doesn't like things to change. Mother threatens to put it in the garbage next time it collapses."

"Boy, I'd like to see it collapse with your dad in — Hi, Hershel!" Ruthie opened the screen door for Hershel, who slouched in slowly, head down, shoulders slumped, and lowered himself to the glider cushion by Pudd'nhead. He sighed deeply and looked at Zoe and Ruthie with mournful eyes.

"What's the matter with you, Gloomy?" asked Zoe. "Are they really going to make you cut your hair at school? That's what I heard."

"I'm not going to cut my hair," said Hershel. He stared at his bare toes and twisted his beads around a button of

his flowered shirt. Then he said, "I've been sitting on the
front steps waiting for it, and then I thought maybe it was
already here, so I came around to see. Is it?"

"Is what here?" asked Zoe. "Nobody brought anything."

"The harpsichord."

Ruthie stopped chewing momentarily. "The *what?*"

"The harpsichord. Mrs. Petrovich's harpsichord. It
was supposed to be here at six o'clock, for the recital. Didn't your mother tell you?"

"She's not here," said Zoe. "Nobody's here except us."

"Why are you interested in the harpsichord?" asked
Ruthie. "Is Mrs. Petrovich going to play in the recital, too?"

Zoe had long been fascinated by the instrument,
smaller than a piano and with a double keyboard, like
an organ, that sat in Mrs. Petrovich's living room. No one,
that she knew of, was ever allowed to touch the keys, black
where a piano's keys were white, except the music teacher.

"Not Mrs. Petrovich," said Hershel. He squirmed and
cleared his throat. "Me."

Ruthie howled with laughter and fell back on the chaise
longue, which collapsed. Zoe bit her lip to keep from
giggling, gave up, and shrieked with Ruthie as she
dragged her from the wreckage.

"Is music your newest thing?" asked Ruthie as she
pulled herself and the chaise longue back together. "Did
you give up on ESP or did Mozart teach you a few things?"

"Do you take music lessons?" asked Zoe, trying to put
things together in her mind as she tried to brace the
broken chair. "I've seen you over at Mrs. Petrovich's
house, but I always thought you came to mow the grass."

"I've taken lessons from her for years," said Hershel. Zoe thought he said it a little proudly, and she hoped they hadn't hurt his feelings by laughing.

"But why don't you ever play for us?" she asked him. "Daddy loves music. You know that. Why didn't you ever say anything about playing?"

Hershel shrugged his shoulders. "Just don't like to play for anybody," he muttered.

"Hershel's shy," Ruthie explained. "But you're supposed to be getting over it, aren't you? Is that why you're playing?"

He shook his head. "Mrs. Petrovich said she wouldn't give me any more lessons until I played in public."

"Boy," said Zoe. "I wish she'd say that to me!"

"You mean you really like it?" asked Ruthie, looking at him as if he had just said casually that he enjoyed sleeping on a bed of nails.

"I like it," he said, and got up. "I'd better get out front to meet the delivery men. They ought to be here soon."

Ruthie jumped up from the floor. "Let's go, Zoe! I wouldn't miss this for anything."

"But Hershel may not want us to be there!" Zoe yelled after her, but Ruthie was gone, off the porch and down the driveway to the front of the house. Zoe followed slowly, and then hurried when she saw Ruthie jumping up and down on the sidewalk and pointing down the block.

Three men were inching down the street, each carrying a corner of the harpsichord, which was made of a striped, exotic-looking wood. They did not seem to find the instrument heavy, but they moved slowly because Mrs. Petrovich kept getting underfoot.

Tiny and very feminine, the music teacher always

dressed in ruffles and laces. She flitted, mothlike, around the three husky moving men, waving a frilly handkerchief and uttering little cries of encouragement or caution in her shrill Slavic accent.

Fascinated, Zoe and Ruthie watched the men lug the instrument up the steps, trying not to trip over Mrs. Petrovich, and into the house. Hershel held the door open for the instrument and all six people, and then followed them into the living room.

The harpsichord was placed in the far end of the living room next to the piano, which dwarfed it. After Mrs. Petrovich had shooed away the dizzy movers, she clapped her hands and piped, "Hershel! Come! You play!" She sat down expectantly and then had to get up again. "Hershel! Where are you, naughty boy? Ah!" She fluttered across the long room to the corner opposite the doors to the hall. Hershel was hiding in the circular alcove formed by the turret, where Mrs. Edwards grew flowers in winter.

He followed Mrs. Petrovich, puppylike, to the harpsichord, and sat at the keyboard. She made a great fuss of moving lamps, raising the lid of the instrument, dusting the keys and Hershel's hair, and seating herself again. Then she clapped her hands again and commanded, "Begin!"

Hershel sighed deeply and began hesitantly, keeping his head bent over the black keys, his long hair covering his face. Zoe threatened to put Ruthie out of the room if she giggled and then sat on the floor out of Hershel's sight, to listen. She was amazed.

He hit many wrong notes and started over twice. But then he seemed to relax and even enjoy what he was doing. The harpsichord twanged and hummed what Zoe thought must be Bach, since she kept hearing two or three melodies in first one hand, then the other, before she lost them in the showers of notes.

When he finished, Zoe clapped and also heard applause from the doorway. She had been too absorbed to notice her mother and father enter quietly.

After Mrs. Petrovich had flitted out of the house, Mr. Edwards insisted that Hershel play the piano for them. "The only way you will get over your stage fright is to play for anybody who'll listen," he said. Zoe thought she hadn't seen her father so happy for a long time.

"I just can't," said Hershel. "Most people just make fun of me." He glanced at Ruthie, who had the grace to look ashamed.

"Those people," said Mr. Edwards, shoving the vacant air aside as if it were a few scorners he would knock aside, "don't matter in our world. Play, Hershel."

Ruthie couldn't resist. "Is Mrs. Petrovich going to make you cut your hair for the recital?" she asked. "She told me to clean my fingernails and leave my gum home!"

Hershel hung his head and his face turned red. "She likes my hair," he confessed. "She thinks it's poetic."

Zoe got Ruthie out of the room in a hurry.

Hershel came the next morning to play the harpsichord, but soon left to escape the confusion in the household. Mrs. Petrovich arrived early with trucks bearing seventy-five folding chairs, five huge baskets of flowers, two punch bowls, and a large box containing cups.

"I thought you said this wouldn't be any trouble," said Mr. Edwards as the family tried to eat a hurried supper before the recital.

Mrs. Edwards pushed back a wisp of hair and hurried

into the kitchen with dishes. "It has gotten a little out of hand," she admitted. "Zoe, you didn't eat a thing."

"I'm too nervous," said Zoe.

"You know that sonatina backward," Mrs. Edwards assured her. "In fact, I think *I* could play it from memory."

"It's Hershel I'm nervous for," Zoe explained. "I just *know* he's going to mess up, or forget, or both. Marcia, you're not going to listen, are you? You'll really *upset* him!"

"I certainly am," said Marcia placidly. "I won't believe he can play until I hear it."

"Well, stay out of sight, at least," Zoe pleaded.

"Zoe, hurry," said her mother as the doorbell sounded. "The programs are on the chair by the front door. Remember, all the little children on the porch outside the French doors. Oh, dear, I hope we have enough chairs."

By seven o'clock the living room was overflowing with proud mothers who spoke in shrill tones about their children's talent and with unhappy fathers who looked as if they would rather be home watching the ball game.

On the porch, where picnic benches had been set up in four rows, nervous, excited children squirmed and yelled. The older students and teen-agers who were to perform, along with their friends, were moved to the stairway in the hall, where they could hear, but not see, the piano. This suited them fine.

At the top of the steps, alone and unaware of the laughing, chattering people below him, sat Hershel. Zoe, standing at the front door giving out programs, glanced up at him whenever she could, but he apparently saw nothing at all.

At the very last minute Zoe saw the red and black

zodiac truck pull up in the driveway. Mr. Zuccini hurried
up the steps, puffing and perspiring, with a square red and
black box, which he carried carefully.

There was only time for a whispered, hurried conversation before Zoe heard Mrs. Petrovich's shrill little welcom-
ing speech.

"Hershel make it all right?" asked Mr. Zuccini. Zoe
pointed to the stairs and Mr. Zuccini looked and frowned.
"Just as I figured. Been nervous as hen in shop all afternoon. Dropped bowl of fish. I sent him home."

Zoe gave him a program, pointing out Hershel's name
at the very end. "That means he's the best," she explained.

Mr. Zuccini shook his head. "Better to let him go first,"
he decided. Then Mrs. Petrovich stood up at the far end
of the living room and clapped her hands.

Zoe looked around the crowded room. "There aren't
any more seats!" she said. "Can you stand against the wall
here in the back? I'll find a kitchen chair for you."

"No matter," he said. "I will be perfect here. Where can
I put box?" He looked around the back of the room, where
there was some room inside the door and against the wall.

Zoe, who knew she should be on the porch with
the class, took the box from him and slid it under a table
against the wall. Mr. Zuccini folded his arms over his
paunch and beamed over the heads of the audience at
Mrs. Petrovich.

Ruthie had saved Zoe a seat beside her on one of the
picnic benches. She slipped into it as the first small pupil
began. Zoe thought he was terrible, but she clapped her
hands as he staggered back out through the French doors
to the porch. Mr. Zuccini, in the back of the room, ap-

plauded as if he had just heard Rubenstein on a good night and called "Bravo!" Heads turned in the audience and people smiled at him and at each other.

"They like him as much as the little kids," Ruthie whispered, as he reacted the same way for the little boy who stumbled through "The Stars and Stripes Forever."

Ruthie played her Schubert Waltz without too many mistakes, and in a few minutes it was Zoe's turn. She walked through the doors to the piano without seeing a single person, and her hands shook as she lifted them to the keyboard. But she remembered to take three deep breaths, and she played the Scarlatti Sonatina fairly well, she thought.

When it was over, Mr. Zuccini's "Bravo! Bravo!" went on until she was back in her seat on the porch.

"Neat-o," said Ruthie.

"If Hershel's that nervous, he'll never make it," Zoe whispered, fanning herself with her program.

"You didn't act nervous," said Ruthie. "Even your father liked it. He actually smiled!"

"Was Daddy out there? I thought he locked himself in the study."

"He came in just as you started and stood at the back, with Mr. Zuccini."

As the program went on toward Hershel's turn, Zoe could stand it no longer. "I'm going around the porch and in the front door," she whispered to Ruthie. "Hershel may have to be carried in."

As she tiptoed through the front hall toward the living-room doors, she saw that Hershel was still staring into space, but now he was wringing his hands. She tried to get his attention, but he didn't see her. Mr. Zuccini made room for her against the wall between himself and the table.

When Sylvia Barnes began her Chopin Ballade, Mr. Edwards appeared at the door and moved to stand beside Mr. Zuccini. As they applauded her performance, Mr. Edwards looked anxiously out the door toward the stairs, and Zoe tiptoed in front of Mr. Zuccini to look, too.

Hershel was making his way down the stairs. It was good that everyone moved for him, because it looked to Zoe as if he would have stepped on someone's hands or feet and never noticed it. But, almost to the bottom of the steps, he did notice someone.

Horrified, Zoe realized that Marcia had been sitting on the steps all along, lost among the crowd. Hershel realized it too, and almost fell down the last two steps. Then he stumbled forward, and Mr. Edwards aimed him toward the harpsichord at the other end of the room. Zoe went back to stand between Mr. Zuccini and the table. Absently, she pulled her braid over her shoulder and began to chew.

As Hershel seated himself at the harpsichord, the murmur that had spread through the audience as they realized that the neighborhood's only hippie was going to perform became a whisper, and then subsided. The audience waited in silence for Hershel to begin.

They waited and waited. Hershel sat at the keyboard as if paralyzed. Zoe saw Mrs. Petrovich, in the front row, begin to finger her hair. Mr. Zuccini, beside Zoe, clasped and unclasped his arms over his paunch. Mr. Edwards cleared his throat.

Still Hershel did not begin.

The audience began to murmur and squirm, obviously embarrassed for the stricken performer. On the porch, a few curious children slid out of their seats and came to the double doors to see what was wrong.

Suddenly Mr. Zuccini leaned over and hissed in Zoe's ear, "Turn over the box!"

Zoe looked up and frowned at him. She couldn't believe he had said what she thought he did. She could hear the murmuring grow louder, and the creaking of chairs as people moved restlessly.

"Turn over box!" Mr. Zuccini said again, quite distinctly.

Zoe put one foot under the table and tipped the red and black box over on its side. The lid fell off slowly.

Out fled an army of white mice.

The results were instant and gratifying. As the tiny mice scampered under chairs and down the aisle, every woman in the room screamed and climbed on her chair. The men, puzzled, stood up or leaned down to see what was causing the trouble. On the porch, children stood on benches to see or rushed as far as the doors, jumping up and down and yelling with delight when they saw the mice.

Zoe saw her father lean his forehead against the door frame, his shoulders shaking with laughter. Mr. Zuccini stood poised, watching the uproar in the room for several seconds. Then he bent down to retrieve the box, pushed his way down the aisle, and stood in the center of the room.

He made himself heard by the sheer volume of his bass voice. "All right, kids!" he yelled toward the French doors. "Penny a mouse!"

Immediately every boy and most of the girls rushed
into the room and dived under chairs, tables, and people.
Mr. Zuccini stood in the middle of the aisle, doling out
pennies and packing mice into the box.

"Thank you, young man. Thank you, little lady. Good
heavens, three? Wonderful!"

The fathers in the audience, now laughing as much as
the teen-agers and children, contributed change. Mothers
began to climb down from their chairs. Mrs. Petrovich
ran in little circles around Mr. Zuccini, piping cries of encouragement to the children and blinking her lashes ad-
miringly at Mr. Zuccini.

At the harpsichord, Hershel finally seemed to realize
what was happening. Zoe saw him shrug his shoulders,
grin, and join the mouse hunt.

Finally calm was restored. When the last visible mouse
had been retrieved and the last penny exhausted, Mr.
Zuccini put the lid on the box firmly and announced, "On
with the music!" He returned to the back of the room,
where he put the box back under the table. Then he
folded his arms and waited for the audience to be seated
again.

Hershel seated himself again. He pushed back his dis-
ordered hair, flexed his fingers, and looked out over the
audience until they quieted. He played the Bach surely
and beautifully, completely relaxed, and with no ap-
parent nervousness. Zoe was so proud she thought she
would burst.

The applause when he finished was deafening, with
Mr. Zuccini's glorious "Bravissimo!" booming over every-
thing. Hershel bowed once and then fled through the
French doors.

Zoe helped her mother serve punch afterward, and watched Mrs. Petrovich accept congratulations.

"Never enjoyed a recital so much," Mr. Edwards told her solemnly, shaking her frail hand.

"Ah, yes, the children are so talented!" she twittered.

Mr. Zuccini seemed to be getting his share of congratulations, too, but he spent most of his time bringing Mrs. Petrovich punch, cookies, napkins, and chairs.

Zoe wandered through the house and out to the porch. The spring night was soft and lovely, and nobody seemed to want to go home. On the front lawn a group of small children, delighted to be up past their bedtimes, shouted as they played hide-and-seek. On the porch groups of teen-agers sat on the steps or straddled the banisters and talked.

Zoe finally found whom she wanted. At the back of the side porch, on the benches where the children had sat, Hershel and Marcia were talking quietly.

Zoe didn't disturb them.

CANCER

June 22 – July 22

1

THE SUMMER VACATION months organized themselves so well that Mrs. Edwards toyed with the idea of giving up her schedules. Everyone except Zoe seemed to have a completely organized vacation. Mr. Edwards was teaching a fairly light class load at the college — "just enough for a little breathing space while he's out of the house," his wife said. Marcia was invited to spend several weeks with Roger's family, along with another girl and boy in her class, at their summer home on Cape Cod. Mr. Edwards did not want her to go.

"You won't be fit to live with when you come back to this old run-down shack," he predicted, waving his arms to indicate the house. "It's bad enough as it is now, hearing these constant comparisons."

"But, Daddy, travel is so broadening! Be a pussy cat!"

It took several days to wear him down, but finally he consented, reluctantly. Marcia spent all her time until her departure at the end of June packing and unpacking and repacking, groaning loudly about the rags she had to wear, all four suitcases of them. In the excitement of going away, she seemed not to think about Hershel at all. Hershel didn't have a house on Cape Cod. The only traveling he would do this summer would be in the Zodiac's delivery truck.

Bob had so much to do at the beginning of the summer that he began to lose his calm, always-in-control air. In addition to studying very hard for his senior exams for admission to a good college in the fall, he had taken a job assisting a construction engineer for the summer. He worked long hours and loved the work, he said, but often he was so tired that he found it difficult to climb down into the hole out by the woods and dig.

He had, however, made enough progress that Zoe could imagine what it would finally look like. At the beginning of the work, she had trouble picturing in her mind what Bob described to her, but now she could see that the oval pond would be only a few inches deep at one end, gradually deepening to a depth of four feet at the other end. The whole length was about ten feet, and around the oval would be a stone wall, sitting height. The rocks Bob dug from the former rock garden were taking shape as he dug. It would be July at least before Hans would have a permanent pool, though.

In the meantime, Mrs. Edwards left her car in the

driveway and Hans swam in a good-sized wading pool borrowed from the Thomases next door. Bob put the pool in the middle of the garage, where it could be drained and cleaned easily enough. Hans could waddle from the garage workshop, where he slept happily among the tools, to the pool without being loose. Still, Zoe knew he needed fresh air. She could hardly wait for the pond to be completed.

Bob also completed the doghouse, but not on schedule. Zoe's birthday came and went, and two more weeks went by before it was finished, but, as everyone decided when Bob called them out to christen it one evening after dinner, it was definitely worth the wait.

"Ready?" he said, with his hand on the doorknob of the workshop. "All eyes closed?"

"Hurry up!" said Zoe. "I can't wait another minute." Bob led the procession in, stumbling and laughing, eyes closed tight.

"Open," he said, when they were inside the workshop.

Zoe could hardly believe what she saw. When she opened her eyes, sitting on the shop floor was a miniature replica of a white Victorian house — gingerbread, turret, porch, roof and all, much like their own house.

"Ye gods!" said Mr. Edwards, examining the shingle roof. "I see now why it took you three months."

Zoe hugged Bob to thank him and examined the porch, which was really a shelter from sun and rain supported by two elaborately carved posts. "It's perfect," she said. "I can see him there now, taking a nap."

"Where is Pudd'nhead, anyway?" asked Marcia, looking around the shop. "He was right beside me when we all closed our eyes to come in."

He was still outside, sound asleep by the door. He had to be shaken to come in and admire his house.

"Don't let him go in," said Marcia, "until we get the house out into the yard. We'll never get him out again."

"Oh, the house is very light, actually," said Bob, lifting it to show her. "And I thought about his sleeping habits when I built the door. It's big enough for Zoe to crawl in if she doesn't eat too much watermelon."

He picked up the house to carry it outside and an indignant Hans quacked from underneath. A feather floated down from the turret.

"He's been sleeping in there for a long time," Bob told them as the duck, still quacking loudly, waddled after them into the yard. "Where do you want it, Zoe?"

Zoe looked around the yard, glad that the twilight kept the pond at the very back of the yard by the woods from being too noticeable, even if her father had worn his glasses outside. "Let's put it under the tree by the garage. No, facing the yard, not the house. Now, Pudd'nhead can lie there and watch everything that happens, can't you, Pudd'nhead? Pudd'nhead?"

They brought him from the garage and shoved him into his house, where he promptly went to sleep with his hind legs sticking out the front door.

"Leave him alone," said Marcia. "He's very tired and he'll figure out that his head should be out."

Hans, with his head cocked to one side, watched the dog go into the house and lie down. Then he waddled through the door, squeezed past the purple hind feet and the white hump of his haunches and made himself comfortable in a back corner. Pudd'nhead, as far as Zoe could see from her rear view, didn't even open an eye.

Zoe stood up and dusted off her hands and knees. "Now there's just one more thing for you to make, Bob," she said.

Mrs. Edwards, thinking she meant the pond, poked her in the ribs and cast her eyes toward Zoe's father.

Zoe shook her head at her mother and went on. "A mousehouse. Ruthie and I are going into the mouse business."

"Ye gods!" said Mr. Edwards. "Who would want one of those things?"

"Practically everybody who heard about the mouse hunt at the recital, that's who," Zoe told him. "I kept seven of the mice, and Mr. Zuccini says they'll have two or three litters a year. It could get out of hand, you know, so I'm going to raise the babies and Ruthie's going to sell them."

"Very enterprising," said Mrs. Edwards. "But I think you got the easier job. After all, you'd be raising them anyway."

"Ruthie doesn't think so," said Zoe. "She's having a ball calling up every boy she can think of to take orders."

The Victorian doghouse was the marvel of the neighborhood for days. Children came from blocks around to admire it, spread the word, and brought their parents. One day a complete stranger knocked on the back door and wanted to buy the plans from Bob.

"We're going to have to set up a schedule of visiting hours," complained Mrs. Edwards, rinsing cups at the kitchen sink. "I can't get a thing done. Everybody who comes to see the doghouse wants to stay and visit. I've used three pounds of coffee this week."

"I agree," said Mr. Edwards. "The traffic has got to cease. I have Important Work to do."

"Maybe we could charge admission," Marcia suggested, "like the stately homes of England."

The stream of curiosity-seekers abated, however, in a week, and Pudd'nhead snoozed in peace, his hind feet outside the house and his head safely inside. He was disturbed only by Hans, who clambered over him several times a day on his way inside for a nap or outside for a swim.

Zoe was alone almost every morning at the beginning of the summer. Bob went to work, Mr. Edwards taught early classes, and Mrs. Edwards and Marcia seemed always to be out shopping for Marcia's trip. Secretly, and a little guiltily, Zoe thought that she would be glad when Marcia left. She liked having the house to herself.

Usually she dug a little deeper in the hole Bob had begun for the pond. Then she splashed with Hans in the wading pool to cool off. Often she just lay idly on the glider on the back porch, watching the Minotaur shinny up the screens, trailing yards of red yarn.

Of course the schedule said for her to clean her room and practice every morning. But with no one in the house, she could bang away at the piano for a few minutes and consider the practicing done. And she spent so little time in her room that all she felt she really had to do was make the bed and carry dirty dishes downstairs. As for the multiplication tables, they annoyed her only occasionally when she couldn't sleep at night.

On a Friday, as she was giving the cricket his corn flakes, Mr. Zuccini called.

"Hi, Zoe. I got problem."

"Not another dog, I hope!"

"No, no. But I have your pet and no way to deliver it. Tragedy! Zodiac truck break down. Want to come get it, or wait till Monday?"

"Oh, I'll come right now!"

"You understand now — pet heavy. You have to come by car."

Mr. Edwards came home at noon, and Zoe strolled casually through the hall to determine his mood. The typewriter in the study was going full blast. Peeping in the door, Zoe saw the morning paper spread open to the editorial page on the table beside the typewriter. Her father's back was to her, but Zoe could hear him mumbling as he typed furiously.

She made him a corned beef sandwich, sliced a large dill pickle, and took a rose from the bouquet on the kitchen table to place on his napkin.

He looked at the tray when she placed it silently on the rocking chair and whirled around in the swivel chair he used when he typed.

"You must want something," he said. "Out with it. I'm busy."

"Are you going downtown for anything today, Daddy?"

"Downtown? Downtown? I haven't been downtown in months. Why should I go downtown? Any more pickles?"

Zoe brought him one on a saucer. "I need a ride to the Zodiac," she told him. "My pet is ready, but Mr. Zuccini's truck broke down. Could you *possibly* take me down?"

"Why don't you walk?" He bit into the second half of the sandwich.

"The pet is too heavy," Zoe told him, and then realized what she had done as he exploded.

"*Too heavy!* Ye gods! What has that Italian Pied Piper come up with this time? How many more pets are there to come, anyway?"

"Only six. Couldn't you take me, please?"

"Out of the question. I have work to do. Ask your mother. Any more pickles?"

Zoe brought him two. "Mother and Marcia went shopping. Who knows when they'll be home?"

He sighed. "Well, we'll see. Let me get some work done, first."

Zoe carried the tray into the kitchen and then managed to go by the study door as often as she could. Finally, after she was breathless and a little dizzy from sighing so loud and so deeply, he stopped typing.

"All right, all right! I'll stop and get your pet. I think I'll just deliver this personally to the editor." He sealed an envelope and tapped it on his desk. He looked extremely pleased. Zoe thought he must have really let the editor have it this time.

"Can I go?"

"No. I want to stop on the way back at the campus. I'll get your pet." He got up and straightened his tie. "It sounds to me as if this one might need inspection first, anyway. Too *heavy*, eh?"

He was gone all afternoon. Marcia and Mrs. Edwards came home, loaded down with boxes and bags, at four o'clock, and disappeared into Marcia's room to try on everything again.

Zoe wandered out to the front porch and sat on the steps, thinking she might just as well have gone swimming. She kept her eyes on the corner next to the Thomases', but she didn't recognize her father's car until it was almost in the driveway. It had crept down the street, and slowed even more as he made the turn before he halted.

"What's wrong with the car?" she asked, running out to meet him.

"Nothing's wrong with the car," he said, as he got out and opened the back door. "Get your mother."

Upstairs the window of Marcia's room flew open and Mrs. Edwards put her head out. "What's the matter with the car?"

"Nothing's the matter with the car!" he repeated, exasperated. "Why must everyone think something is the matter?"

Marcia's head appeared at the window, too. "Daddy, you never go that slow in the *garage,* much less down the street!"

"Come and help me carry these things in," he called toward the window.

"Can't Zoe do it? We're trying on."

"Too many," he answered. "And too heavy."

In the back seat Zoe could see several small packages, some of them very oddly shaped, and one large, oblong one which was propped on the back seat with textbooks and papers so it was level.

Mrs. Edwards hurried down the front steps and stopped in the middle of the yard under the pine tree. "John Edwards," she said, with her hands on her hips, "you got another ticket! And you *know* what the judge said last time!"

Mr. Edwards plucked the telltale pink slip from the dashboard and put it hastily in his jacket pocket.

"This is *not* a speeding ticket," he said. "It's for going too slow."

"Too slow!" said Zoe. "I don't believe it!"

"Neither did I until the policeman wrote it out," said her father. "Ridiculous law, anyway! I'll write a letter on it as soon as I get the fish settled." He began piling Zoe's arms high with packages and then turned to Marcia, who had followed her mother out.

"Did you say fish?" asked Zoe.

"Fish," he answered. "Helen, you take that end as I push it across the seat to you."

Mrs. Edwards staggered slightly as the package slid to her waiting hands. "Good heavens, what *is* this?"

"Careful," said Mr. Edwards, as he slid across the back seat, holding his end of the red and black package. "You'll spill the water."

"Dear," said Mrs. Edwards, using her kindergarten-teacher voice, "it would be easier to pour out most of the water so it wouldn't be so heavy and refill the aquarium, if that's what it is, when we get it inside."

"Can't," he answered. "The water is *seasoned*. The fish will die if you put them in water that hasn't been properly treated and settled."

They crossed the yard, climbed the steps, and finally reached the front hall. "Where's it going?" gasped Mrs. Edwards.

"In *my* room," Zoe said promptly.

"Let's put it in the turret," said Marcia. "It would look nice with the plants."

"Well, hurry up and decide," said her mother. "This thing is *heavy!*"

"Probably the seasoning," suggested Marcia. "On

second thought, we could watch the fish better in the family room . . ."

"It is going," said Mr. Edwards definitely, "in the study."

2

ZOE'S FATHER was hooked, no doubt about it.

She spent all evening in the study helping him prepare the aquarium for its two occupants, adjusting the thermometer, installing the filter, mounting the fluorescent light, and listening to him lecture knowledgeably about Siamese fighting fish.

"Actually, *Betta splendens* is the correct name," he said.

"Where did you learn so much about fish?" Zoe asked.

"Why, this afternoon at the Zodiac, from Mr. Zuccini."

"But — you must have spent the whole afternoon there!"

"I did." Mr. Edwards stepped back to judge the effect of the plants waving in the clear water. Suddenly he looked startled. "Ye gods! I never did go see the editor."

Zoe climbed on the arm of the swivel chair to reach a dusty F volume of the encyclopedia. The chair tilted precariously and she had to cling to a shelf to keep from falling.

"Careful!" said Mr. Edwards. "You'll knock dust in the aquarium. I don't know *why* your mother can't seem to schedule time to dust this room."

He lifted Zoe down and together they read the article

on tropical fish. There was very little about Siamese fighting fish.

"We need a good book or two on fish," Mr. Edwards said. "Next time I'm at the Zodiac I'll check the collection. You should see all the fish down there, Zoe. Black-finned colossoma, Congo characin, blue limia — "

"I saw them all," Zoe reminded him. "I even gave away goldfish at the Grand Opening, remember?"

"Goldfish!" he said scornfully. "Goldfish are for amateurs! Now these, *these* fish are for true connoisseurs, like we are."

They bent over the tank to watch the two Siamese fighting fish, which faced each other, almost nose to nose, through a glass partition. The fish were two inches long, a dark, dull color, and they had waving fins on their backs, bellies, and tails. As they saw each other through the glass, their colors changed to the brightest of blues and scarlets, the fins enlarged to three times their normal size, and the fish lashed themselves back and forth in the water.

"If we took out the partition, would they really fight?" asked Zoe.

"Rip each other to bloody shreds," her father whispered back.

"Let's try it."

"Zoe! How bloodthirsty!" Mr. Edwards drew back from his daughter and glared at her.

"Just kidding," Zoe told him, and laughed.

They watched the fish drift away from each other. When each fish lost sight of the enemy on the other side of the glass partition, he lost his bright color and his fins contracted again.

"Yang and Yin," said Mr. Edwards.

"What?" said Zoe. "Is that what you're calling the fish?"

"No, but it's not a bad idea," he said.

"What does it mean?"

"Look it up."

The Y volume read:

> Yang and Yin: In Chinese philosophy, terms used to represent the active and passive forces of the universe. Yang represents light and activity, and Yin represents darkness and passiveness. From the interaction of the two, all things begin.

There was even a diagram which looked like two fish to Zoe:

And they certainly did make things happen, as Zoe found out later in the week, when she stood on the back porch in swimming suit and beachrobe.

"Don't take off your wet suit," her mother said as she ran through the kitchen with a mop and a bucket. "You may need it."

Zoe could see the water from the hall, even before she waded into the study. Mrs. Edwards stood, water sloshing over her bare toes, wringing out the mop at the open window. The garden hose hung limply over the sill, dripping water on a pile of *Harper's* magazines.

"Welcome to Marineland," said Mrs. Edwards bitterly. "Get a towel."

Mr. Edwards sat in the middle of the flood, his feet tucked up on the rungs of his rocking chair, a sheepish look on his face. All around him floated clippings, papers, pamphlets, and letters.

In every available space in the room, on bookcases, tables, desk, and swivel chair, were aquariums, either empty or partly filled with water except for one, which was full to the brim. Zoe counted ten of them.

She brought towels from the hall closet and silently handed one to her father.

"Don't give *him* one," Mrs. Edwards snapped. "*He* won't help."

Zoe thought he looked as if he might, but she didn't say so. After she sopped up water for a few minutes, she asked timidly, "What happened?"

Mrs. Edwards flung the garden hose out the window. "Your father went shopping," she said. "And he thought he'd fill the aquariums the easy way. And he forgot to turn off the hose!" She wiped her sweaty forehead and glared at her husband, who smiled sickly.

"I was doing — " he began.

"John Edwards, if you tell me you were doing Important Work I shall *scream!*" Mrs. Edwards shook her mop at him.

Zoe giggled at her father, who was cringing in his rocking chair. "This place looks more like the Zodiac's fish department than the study."

"More like twenty thousand leagues under the sea! Mop!"

At dinner Zoe's father was still subdued. He ate his pork chop quietly as Marcia and Bob went into howls of laughter at the flood in the study.

Mrs. Edwards watched him picking at his food. "Something wrong with the food, I suppose?" she challenged him.

"I didn't say — "

"Well, don't. If you don't like what we eat, you can find another boarding house."

"But aren't there any fish in all those tanks?" asked Bob. He had been to inspect the wrecked study for himself.

"Not yet," Zoe explained. "The water has to season for a week."

"I'd like to season it all right," said her mother grimly. "With salt and pepper."

Mr. Edwards gradually got over his humiliating experience, and by the time Mr. Zuccini delivered the fish for all the aquariums, the dinner-table conversation was awash with talk of cichlids, acaras, zebra barbs, and one-lined pencilfish. Zoe and her father argued about dH and pH, discussed temperature control, considered aquascaping in depth.

"Do you realize," said Mr. Edwards one evening, "that one of the most beautiful words in our language is just a fish food?"

"Are we going to have the Fourth of July picnic this year or is it the Thomases' turn?" mused Mrs. Edwards.

"Daphnia," said Mr. Edwards. "Isn't that a beautiful word? I wonder why we didn't name one of our girls Daphnia."

"I'd rather be Marcia," said Marcia.

"I'd rather be Debbie," said Zoe.

"I'd better call Peggy Thomas," said Mrs. Edwards. "I've forgotten to put the picnic on the schedule."

Her family put down their spoons and stared at her.

"Well, it's all these fish," she said defensively. "Ever since your father decided he was Jacques Costeau, things have been off schedule."

"I wish you'd get the daphnia out of the refrigerator, Daddy," Marcia complained. "It smells awful!"

"Have you seen the white worms growing in the basement?" Bob asked.

"Worms? In the basement? Good heavens, I was down there ironing this morning!" Marcia lifted her feet to her chair rung and looked underneath for possible wriggling creatures.

"Couldn't we talk about something else?" asked Zoe. "My ice cream is beginning to taste like sardines."

"Brine shrimp," corrected her mother. "There are five pounds in the freezer. Unwrapped."

"Japanese carp," said Mr. Edwards.

"Pay no attention to him," said Mrs. Edwards, twirling her forefinger beside her temple. "Marcia, are you packed and ready to go?"

"I'm all ready," said Marcia. "The Wilsons are picking me up early."

Mr. Edwards put down his spoon. "That's it!" he said excitedly. "I can have Japanese carp! Bob, how much trouble do you think it would be to dig out the old pond?"

His family put down their spoons and stared at him.

"Why, not much trouble," said Bob finally. "Tell you what. Let me dig around a little out there in the morning to get the lay of the land and I'll let you know."

"Magnificent!" was Mr. Zuccini's pronouncement when he saw the work Bob had done while he was getting the lay of the land.

"Isn't this going to be a fine place for carp?" Mr. Edwards asked proudly. "And it's been no trouble at all! Why, just look at all the work we've done in just a couple of days."

Waist-deep in the hole, his shirtless son straightened from his shovel and wiped sweat from his brow. Mr. Zuccini winked at him.

"You got good helper here, Mr. Edwards. Hey, Bob, you want Hershel to help? He have plenty of time soon, when I go back to old country."

"You're going to Italy, Mr. Zuccini?" asked Mr. Edwards.

"First trip back in many years! Shop be closed for a while, though. Plenty of time to order fish, though." He looked around at the pond again. "Wonderful idea, Mr. Edwards! Nobody but you think of fixing up old pond!"

3

FOR AS MANY YEARS as Zoe could remember, the Edwards and Thomas families had shared a Fourth of July picnic in one back yard or the other. It was the Edwards's turn this summer. Zoe asked Ruthie to come, since Tooty Thomas was bringing Elmer, as usual.

"Don't you want to ask a girl?" Mrs. Edwards asked Bob. "It seems as if something is missing with Marcia gone."

"Who has time for girls?" Bob demanded. "That pond and the mouse house and a full-time job are all I can handle!"

"Why don't you ask Mr. Zuccini?" suggested Mr. Edwards.

"What a good idea! He must be lonesome all alone over that shop! You're sure he hasn't left for Italy yet?"

Mr. Zuccini had not left, and he possibly was not as lonely as Mrs. Edwards thought. He arrived in the back yard on the evening of the Fourth with three watermelons, four bottles of Italian wine, and Mrs. Petrovich.

"I bring a friend," he said, bowing grandly as he presented the wine and melons. "You not mind, I was sure."

"Of course not!" said Mrs. Edwards. "We're delighted to have Klara. The most interesting things happen when she is here."

Ruthie and Zoe, who had watched the grownups talk from across the yard, eyed Mr. Zuccini and Mrs. Petrovich speculatively as they strolled around the lawn admiring the flowers and the pond.

"Do you think — ?" began Zoe.

"Absolutely," said Ruthie. "Look at them. The owl and the pussy cat."

"Or the lion and the lamb," Zoe giggled, watching Mrs. Petrovich's frothy dress and lacy handkerchief flutter about Mr. Zuccini.

After dinner, when the first fireflies began to twinkle, Zoe and Ruthie, Tooty and Elmer lay on the grass across the lawn from the doghouse, watching Mr. Thomas set up his fireworks display.

"Fireworks!" twittered Mrs. Petrovich. "I shall be terrified."

Mr. Zuccini, bulky as he was, and as full of watermelon, wine, and hamburgers, bounded out of his chair to stand beside her.

"Where did you get the fireworks?" asked Mrs. Edwards. "Aren't they illegal in this state?"

"Yes," replied Mr. Thomas. "A friend brought them to me. But it'll be perfectly all right here in the back yard."

"But the police — "

"Go right ahead, Harry," said Mr. Edwards. "That is a ridiculous law, anyway."

Zoe, listening to their conversation, propped herself up on one elbow and said to Elmer, "Daddy is a law unto himself."

"Yeah, I heard," Elmer answered lazily. "Is it true he makes speeches in traffic court every month?"

The grownups and Bob went to sit far back in the yard by the pond to watch the fireworks, and Zoe and her friends stayed where they were, lying on their backs in the grass, facing Mr. Thomas's display in the center of the yard, but at a safe distance from it. Tooty's father darted about with rockets and Roman candles, busily lining them up on their stick launching pads for blastoff.

From her position in the grass, Zoe had to look through the lines of rockets to see the doghouse directly across from her and behind Mr. Thomas.

"I think I'll put Hans in the garage for safety," she said, and, taking a leftover bun from the picnic table near them, she ran across the yard and lured him into the garage by walking backward and holding out the bread before him. The duck quacked indignantly at being exiled when she shut the door on him. Before she came back across the yard, Zoe chained Pudd'nhead, who didn't wake up long enough to notice, to the post of his porch.

The fireworks display began with an unexpected string of firecrackers, hissing, popping, showering sparks in the center of the yard. The children covered their ears and screamed with delight.

As the sputtering died down, Zoe heard a sound she had never heard before. It took her a minute to realize that Pudd'nhead was growling.

"The noise hurts his ears," said Zoe. "I think I'd better put him in the garage too."

But she was too late. Mr. Thomas, his face lit eerily by the sizzling fuses, waved her back to her seat on the grass and set up the first rocket.

Sputtering, whooshing upward, trailing a shower of sparks, the rocket exploded above them with a deep boom. A gorgeous, slowly expanding spray of blue streaks fanned out against the night sky. A red one followed, and another blue one, as fast as Mr. Thomas could light the fuses. Dancing about in the flashing lights, he looked like a diabolical cannoneer.

Ruthie and Zoe tried to yell at each other above the noise, gave up, and watched the show with their hands over their ears.

BOOM! BOOM! BOOM! Great splashes of red and blue and white lit the sky over the yard. Zoe, shifting positions to lie flat on her back so she could see better, suddenly sat up abruptly and stared at something unfamiliar moving directly across the yard. It was hard to see in the dark, and Mr. Thomas kept crossing her path of vision, but in the next flashes of light, Zoe made out what the moving object was.

The doghouse was bouncing across the grass.

Pudd'nhead, apparently terrified by the lights and the noise, was determined to escape. Not only was he on his feet, which was unusual enough, but he was digging in with his powerful haunches, straining his chain taut, and pulling with all his sixty-five pounds on the plywood doghouse. And it began to move. Zoe watched from across the yard, horrified.

Howling, the old dog gathered momentum and headed for the driveway, dragging the house behind him. No one else seemed to see. Ruthie, Elmer, and Tooty were flat on their backs. Zoe shook Ruthie and yelled in her ear, but Ruthie only nodded and pointed to the sky. The grownups were too far back in the yard to see, and their eyes were on the sky, too.

Zoe jumped up and ran across the yard toward the driveway. Mr. Thomas, intent on lighting as many fuses as possible at once, was too absorbed to notice her as she flashed by.

Pudd'nhead reached the driveway, where the surface was smoother. He was able to trundle along the slight downhill slope at a good rate. Zoe reached the corner of the back porch just as the doghouse went by it. As dog and doghouse disappeared around the house, she had time only to lunge into the darkness and grab frantically at the turret.

She landed draped across the shingles of the doghouse roof and hung on. Scrambling madly, she managed to climb aboard and straddle the roof. As her added weight and the downhill slope of the driveway added momentum to Pudd'nhead's headlong flight, Zoe clung to the turret.

The driveway was darker than the back yard, since the house cut off most of the flashing lights from the sky. Behind her Zoe could vaguely hear voices shouting and feet pounding on the driveway pavement. The dog, still howl-

ing, was moving faster and faster toward the street.

They passed the porch beside the living room and the streetlamp cast light on the driveway from the front of the house to the street. Zoe screamed at Pudd'nhead to stop as she saw someone walking directly toward them in the driveway. Everything happened so fast that she only noticed the flash of gold buttons on a dark jacket before dog and doghouse plowed into the policeman.

She fell off. The doghouse tipped over in the other direction. She lay on the concrete, stunned for a moment, before she became aware of voices around her. Arms helped her to sit up. Someone yelled in her ear for her not to move anymore. Hands felt her body for broken bones. In the back yard, rockets exploded madly.

As her vision cleared, she saw Bob righting the doghouse and Mrs. Edwards bending over Pudd'nhead, who lay tangled in his chain, still howling unhappily. Mr. Zuccini and Mrs. Petrovich were helping the policeman rise.

Zoe got up slowly and picked up the policeman's hat from the driveway. Mr. Edwards was gathering up his flashlight, his stick, and his black book.

"Officer, are you all right?" yelled Mr. Edwards over the noise of the rockets, the shouting of all the people in the driveway, and the piteous howling of the dog.

The policeman, rubbing his forehead slowly, fought off Mrs. Petrovich's lacy handkerchief with one hand.

An earsplitting blast from the back yard delayed his reply. Then, taking out a pencil, he opened his black book and said, "Am I all right? Mister, have you ever been run down by a girl driving a doghouse? I may never be all right again." As he began to write, he shook his head and said, "They'll never believe this down at the station house."

In the back yard, blissfully unaware that his audience had deserted him, Mr. Thomas managed to light five fuses at once and sent up a last, glorious burst of spectacular color.

LEO

●

July 23 – August 22

Working on weekends and in the evenings when the weather was cooler, Bob finished the pond by the middle of July.

Zoe, carrying her duck, went out to show it to her father. He surveyed the oval, rock-ledged pool surrounded by freshly sodded grass and shaded by the big maple, and pronounced it good.

"I think I'll bring my chaise longue out here from the porch," he decided. "And the picnic table. I shall sit and look at the woods while I work, like Thoreau."

So Bob lugged the heavy table from the middle of the yard and the antiquated chaise longue from the porch.

"We may as well bring the typewriter out, too," decided Mr. Edwards, settling cautiously into his favorite chair.

While Bob was getting the typewriter, Zoe asked timidly, "Can we put the duck in? I can't hold him much longer. He smells the water."

"Of course, of course!" Mr. Edwards waved his hand generously toward the pond. "He'll be very decorative."

Relieved that it had been so easy to talk him into it, Zoe put Hans down at the shallow end where the rock ledge ended. The duck waded in immediately, quacking with low, short contented sounds.

Zoe watched him when he was in full sail at the far end of the pond. "Isn't he beautiful?" she said. "We should have a picture of that."

"Just wait for the *pièce de résistance*," said Mr. Edwards.

He meant the Japanese carp, of course, which Mr. Zuccini was to deliver that day. They had been imported at great expense. Mrs. Edwards, still bristling when she remembered the flood in the study, had objected vehemently to them.

"If you *ever* complain about how much this poor dog costs to feed, after bringing those goldfish all the way from Japan on a plane, I'll take *your* meals right off the schedule," she had told her husband.

"Goldfish? Goldfish? These are not goldfish!"

"Aren't carp those muddy-looking fish at the bottom of moats?" Zoe had asked.

"No, no. That's a type of carp, but not like the ones I'm getting. These are more like — well, like goldfish."

"But you said — " Mrs. Edwards had groaned.

"Never mind, you'll see," said her husband.

They *are* like giant goldfish, Zoe thought, as she watched Mr. Zuccini lower the bucket containing them into the pond later in the day. The big fish, stippled and spotted and gorgeously colored, swam to the top of the bucket and out into the pond, where they went immediately to the bottom.

Zoe stood up to look down into the water. "I can't see them," she said. "Do they always stay at the bottom?"

"Run get bread from truck," Mr. Zuccini instructed her. "They come up to eat."

Zoe brought the bag of stale bread and threw a few pieces in the water. The carp rose, their mouths round as half dollars, and gobbled the food greedily. Hans, who had been floating lazily at the far end of the pond, paddled over curiously. Dipping his bill practically into a fish's mouth, he sampled the bread and quacked for more. Zoe threw him another piece and he raced a fish for it. The fish won.

"Get that duck away from my carp! Shoo! Go away!" Mr. Edwards flapped his arms wildly at the duck, who paid no attention at all.

"Shoo! Zoe, get him out."

"Plenty for all," said Mr. Zuccini, heaving a piece of bread at Hans.

"Zoe!"

"But, Daddy, it's his pond, too!"

"Well, shoo him over to the other side."

Zoe coaxed Hans away from the fish and sat on the rock ledge, feeding him bread. Mr. Edwards fed his carp tenderly while Mr. Zuccini admired the pond, the woods, the house, and the doghouse.

"Wonderful home you have here," he said, as he did every time he came. "Sure you don't want to sell? I may need nice house someday soon."

"Not this month," said Mr. Edwards. He glanced at Hans, who was turning tentatively toward the fish again, and added, "Where else could I put all these animals you keep bringing?"

Mr. Zuccini stood up from his seat on the ledge and slapped his forehead with his palm. "I forgot! Zoe, I brought your pet."

Zoe jumped up, duck forgotten. "Is it in the truck?"

He shook his head and winked at her. "Nope! You have to find!"

"You *hid* the pet?"

"Not exactly," he answered mysteriously. "You look around. You find. When you do, call me about food for her, or if you have questions. Remember, I leave tomorrow for Italy, so call before then."

After she said her good-byes to Mr. Zuccini, Zoe began to search immediately. There was no pet in the house or the garage, and although she gave up her afternoon swim to look, she found no sign of either animal or red and black Zodiac box.

After dinner, as she was feeding Pudd'nhead, Hershel strolled into the back yard from the driveway. He wore raggedly fringed jeans and was barefoot. Around his neck hung the biggest peace medallion Zoe had ever seen.

"Hi, Zoe. Mrs. Edwards said your father was out here."

"He's out by the pond. Come and see it!"

"Welcome to Walden Pond," said Mr. Edwards as Zoe and Hershel approached his chaise longue.

"If you had a beard, you'd look like Thoreau sitting in

his woods watching the birds," Hershel said. "Any loons out here?"

"Depends on what kind you mean," said Mr. Edwards, glaring at Hans. "Sit down, Hershel."

Zoe sat on the grass at her father's feet. "Why didn't you come and help with the pond?" she asked Hershel, as he seated himself on the ledge of the pond. "Marcia's gone all summer. It's safe."

"I've been busy," said Hershel. He let the peace medallion dangle from his fingers. "Marching."

"You can get all the peace you want right here by this pond," said Mr. Edwards. "I don't know why I never thought about this before! I may even catch up on my work out here."

"I see Zoe in the pond," said Hershel suddenly.

"What?" Zoe jumped up and ran to look where he was pointing. "Where?"

"Right by the edge. That round rock. See?"

The rock had four legs, a tail, and a head, all of which disappeared as soon as Zoe lifted it from the water.

"You found it," said her father mournfully. "I was hoping it would wander off into the woods."

"You mean you knew it was here?"

"Mr. Zuccini put it in the water when you went for the bread."

Zoe inspected the turtle's painted shell closely. Across the curved carapace the letters Z-O-E were painted. The word was formed of tiny, delicately stenciled violets and leaves.

"Some painted turtle," said Zoe, delighted with the pet. "I guess we name her Violet."

"How do you know it's a she?" asked her father.

"I heard Mr. Zuccini call it *her*," Zoe answered. "And anyway, who ever heard of a boy named Violet?" She watched Violet crawl back toward the rocky, shallow edge of the pond. "Is Violet literary enough for you, Daddy?"

"Of course it is," said Hershel. "Must be dozens of poems with violets in them."

"For example," said Mr. Edwards, in his professorial voice,

> *Such a starved bank of moss*
> *Till that May morn,*
> *Blue ran the flash across;*
> *Violets were born.*"

"Or," said Hershel, after a moment's thought,

> *The deep blue eyes of Springtime*
> *Peer from the grass beneath;*
> *They are the tender violets*
> *That I will twine in a wreath.*"

"Very good," said Mr. Edwards. "Hershel, you've been reading as well as marching this summer."

"I know one," said Zoe.

"Let's hear it."

"Roses are red, violets — "

"Ye gods!"

Zoe called Ruthie early the next morning to come over and see the turtle and the new mouse house, which had taken Bob only a day or so.

"Neat-o!" was Ruthie's verdict. "It's not as pretty as the

doghouse, but it's sure practical. Wow! Look at those mice go!"

The mouse house was simply a large, square wooden box on low legs. Bob had divided it into three floors by using a fine wire mesh. The Seven Dwarfs could run from floor to floor by means of a spiral ramp, and they apparently loved the exercise because they seemed to be in constant motion from the time Zoe introduced them to their new home. The box had a hinged lid, which could be raised to put food on the top floor, and the bottom floor slid out for cleaning, as Zoe demonstrated to Ruthie. On the middle floor Zoe had made an entertainment center, where the mice could run around inside a wheel, admire themselves in a mirror, or play hide-and-seek in a maze.

"Mr. Zuccini said we should have a litter of babies any day now," Zoe said, as she showed Ruthie how the house could be covered with a cloth so that it looked like a table.

"I sure hope so," said Ruthie. "I haven't talked to any cute boys in ages."

"You see plenty of them at the pool every afternoon."

"I know, but I need an *excuse*," Ruthie explained. "I wouldn't want them to think I'm fast."

Through the window overlooking the back yard came the sound of the dinner gong, three times. Zoe climbed off her bed immediately and headed for the door. The gong sounded again.

Ruthie followed her down the stairs. "Why is your father ringing the gong? It's too early for lunch."

"He got tired of coming back to the house every time he needed something. When he rings three times, I'm supposed to go out and see what he wants."

"You people spoil that man," Ruthie said, as they

turned into the kitchen. "Why can't he come and get things for himself?"

"*Daddy?*" asked Zoe incredulously. "Do something somebody else can do?"

The gong sounded again as they stopped at the kitchen sink for a drink of water. "Boy, is he impatient!" said Ruthie.

"The neighbors are all confused about it," Zoe said. "The first day he did it they kept calling to see why we were having dinner at two o'clock in the afternoon. And Tooty's dad came over to see if there was an emergency."

Ruthie opened the screen door. "Like the fire bell in olden days. Zoe, what is he *doing?*"

Zoe broke into a run when she looked out toward the pond. Her father was standing on the rock ledge, throwing stones at the duck.

"Stop! Stop!" she screamed as she ran. "Daddy, you'll kill him!"

"Get that cannibal out of my pond!" shouted Mr. Edwards. "He ate one of my carp." He hurled another pebble at Hans, who quacked and swam in little circles at the opposite side from Mr. Edwards.

Ruthie arrived breathlessly and took in the situation. "Don't worry about a thing, Zoe," she said calmly, beginning a bubble. "His aim is terrible."

"Daddy, stop throwing rocks and get down! He won't come out with you there."

Mr. Edwards climbed off the ledge and walked toward the woods. Hans swam madly to the shallow end, waded out, and half waddled, half flew to the doghouse. He turned around once to quack before he walked over

Pudd'nhead's rump and inside to safety. He didn't come out until dinner time.

Mr. Edwards threw bread to the carp and counted mouths.

"Six! You see?" said Zoe.

"Five," said Mr. Edwards.

"Six," said Ruthie. "You can't count much better than you can throw, Mr. Edwards." She smiled sweetly and added, "Can you say your twelves?"

Zoe's father glared at her, speechless.

Zoe said, "Daddy, there are still six fish in that pond. Hans wouldn't hurt one! And if you ever throw rocks at my duck again, I'll run away from home."

"Fine. Take your duck with you. And your friend who's so smart."

"I will," said Zoe. "Come on, Ruthie."

Halfway back to the house, she turned and called to him, "And you'll miss me when I'm gone. There won't be anybody to answer your silly old gong!"

They left him standing there, his mouth as wide and round as one of the six carps' mouths.

VIRGO

August 23 – September 22

Mr. EDWARDS HAD SAID that Marcia wouldn't be fit to live with when she came home from her vacation on Cape Cod, but he couldn't have been more mistaken. Marcia was so considerate and sweet that Zoe was ashamed of having wished she would never come home.

Marcia did her chores without complaint and paid back Zoe for the days she had owed her since spring. She volunteered to answer the gong whenever she was at home, and she drove Zoe and Ruthie to the pool with her for their afternoon swim.

She loved the pond by the woods, and spent a good deal of time with her father there. She even did some of his

typing for him, seated in the shade of the big maple, with
Pudd'nhead beside her. The old dog was so glad Marcia
was back that he stirred long enough to drag himself out
of the house and across the long yard. Zoe was a little
jealous, but her sister was being so kind to her that she
tried not to show it.

Something had happened to Marcia while she was
away, but Zoe didn't know what it was. She seemed much
more contented to stay at home. Roger called only once
the week she came home, and she didn't go out with
him at all. Zoe was very curious. And so was everyone
else.

"If this is what living among the idle rich does for you,"
Mr. Edwards told her one day as he watched her typing
industriously on the picnic table, "I'd like to send *somebody else* to try it." He looked over his glasses at Zoe and
grinned wickedly.

Zoe glared right back at him. "I second the motion!"
she said, and threw a crust of toast to Hans.

Mr. Edwards still refused to admit that he had
miscounted his carp, and added insult to injury by teasing her mercilessly about Hans.

"Just you wait until Thanksgiving, duck!" he would yell
every time he passed the doghouse.

Or, "an eye for an eye!" he would threaten as the duck
paddled near the carp.

Now, watching Hans float peacefully in the hot sunshine glaring on the pond, he said, "That duck certainly
is getting fat and juicy. I can hardly wait!"

Marcia stopped typing and laughed at her father.
"Stop teasing Zoe," she told him. "She believes every
word you say!"

"Good," said Mr. Edwards. "She may as well be prepared. I have a Biblical revenge all planned for that duck."

Exasperated, Zoe got up from the ledge and reminded him, "Marcia counted six carp, too. You kill that duck and you're a murderer."

Marcia got up and planted a pink kiss on her father's forehead. "I won't let him hurt Hans," she said, as she ruffled his hair.

Mr. Edwards looked at his older daughter speculatively as he wiped off the lipstick. "I certainly would like to know," he said, "what made you decide this isn't such a bad place to live after all."

Marcia went to sit on the ledge and trailed her hand in the water. She sat silently for a minute and then said, "I never thought this was a bad place to live. I guess I just didn't see the bad things about other places — and other families."

"Like what?" asked her father.

"Oh, I don't know. Like — being bored with bridge every day, day after day, and nothing but talk about cars and clothes and gossip — I don't know." She stood up and looked at her watch. "Come on, Zoe, pool's open. Race you to the house!"

They stayed late at the pool. Mrs. Edwards was standing at the kitchen sink shredding lettuce as Zoe followed Marcia onto the back porch. The sound of the piano by the open French doors drifted to them from around the house.

Mrs. Edwards put down her knife. "Hershel's here. He brought your pet, Zoe, since Mr. Zuccini is away." She looked at Marcia a little uncertainly and her eyebrows went up as she added, "Your father asked him to stay for dinner."

Marcia said only, "Sounds as if he's making him sing for it," and went upstairs to change her clothes.

"The pet is on the front porch," Mrs. Edwards said. "Around by the turret, I think. Hershel was going to leave it and not come in, but your father caught him."

Zoe didn't wait to change her clothes. She tiptoed through the front hall and out to the porch, still wearing her beachcoat over her damp swimming suit. There was a large package sitting beside the turret wall, not far from the French doors. In the living room her father was listening to Hershel play, and Zoe had to work slowly to get the red and black paper off the package soundlessly.

It was a wire cage. Inside Zoe saw a shoebox turned upside down to form a house for something. Opening the top of the cage, she lifted the shoebox curiously.

She uncovered a tiny, long-haired guinea pig — a cavy, she knew they were called. She remembered the short-haired one that Ruthie's brother had once owned, but she had never seen a guinea pig like this. It was three colors — black to his middle, reddish-brown around his belly, and white to his rear.

Zoe picked him up carefully, hardly able to tell one end from the other because of all the silky hair that completely covered his face and flowed past his feet. She sat down and leaned against the turret, holding him against her terrycloth beachcoat. He nuzzled a button and snuggled against her. The amazing long hair whorled from a crooked part in the center of his back, stood up in wavy tufts on his head, and curled over her fingers as she stroked him. When she leaned forward to pull her braid over her shoulder, the cavy nibbled it experimentally.

She held him a long time, leaning against the turret and listening to Hershel play. As the guinea pig nuzzled her chin and ears, Zoe realized that this was the first pet she could actually pick up and *love*.

When the dinner gong sounded and the music stopped, Zoe put the little animal back in his shoebox and closed the top of the cage. As she walked slowly through the house to dinner, she wished Mr. Zuccini were where she could call him and thank him.

The timid, good-natured cavy was the first pet that the whole family loved unreservedly. He seemed content to stay in his cage and munch lettuce leaves and carrots most of the time, although he would oink urgently to be picked up whenever anyone came near the cage on the back porch. Zoe discovered that he could be let out of the cage on the back porch, because the one step up into the kitchen made an effective barrier. The cavy soon had the run of the porch, where he spent most of his time exploring corners or hiding under the glider. If he came across the Minotaur's red leash in his exploring, he usually nibbled it in two, but since most of the ball of yarn was usually unwound across the porch floor and up the screen, no harm was done.

Best of all, he liked to graze in the back yard. Zoe took him out after dinner every night, when the sun was gone, and he explored the whole yard. Although he was tiny, he could move amazingly fast, and Zoe often had to rescue him from under a bush or from the marigold bed near the back porch. When he completely disappeared, she always looked there. Marigold leaves were definitely his favorite food.

"If I turn my back for one minute, he's gone," she told Ruthie one evening as they lay on the grassy slope near the pond, listening to the late-summer cicadas and watching the fireflies come out in the twilight.

"There he is, under the chaise longue," said Ruthie. "I hope that thing doesn't collapse on him."

Zoe crawled under the chair and retrieved the cavy. Ruthie helped her brush the twigs from the long coat. "How does he get along with Hans and Pudd'nhead?" she asked.

"Hans is scared to death of him," Zoe told her, "but Pudd'nhead seems to like him. Of course, nothing bothers Pudd'nhead."

"Except fireworks."

"Except fireworks. And he hasn't moved since then."

Ruthie caught the guinea pig as he darted for the shrubs on the other side of the yard. "He's going to get into trouble that way. If he ever got into the woods, you'd never find him."

Zoe took her pet and held it in her lap. "I'll take good care of him," she said. "I won't let anything happen to him."

"Did you name him yet?"

Zoe shook her head. "We can't find a good name. Daddy says there just aren't any literary references to guinea pigs."

"Oh, you'll think of something," said Ruthie. "Hey, speaking of animals, aren't those mice *ever* going to have babies?"

Zoe sighed. "I don't know what's wrong! Mr. Zuccini said it was bound to happen any time."

Ruthie sat up and gazed at the pond. "Well, I wish they'd hurry. Gee, Zoe, your turtle's really grown!"

"Violet?" Zoe raised herself up on her elbows to look where Ruthie pointed. "You know, I think you're right! I didn't even notice. That's odd. I thought turtles stayed the same size for ages."

Next morning when Zoe took Violet her tomato at breakfast time, she thought the turtle had grown more. It couldn't be, she thought. Must be that she looks different in the daytime.

A day later the turtle was still larger, there was no doubt about it.

"Ye gods!" said her father when she showed him. He put on his glasses for a closer look as Zoe picked up Violet. A week ago, she had just covered Zoe's hand when she

sat on it. Now Zoe had to spread her fingers to hold her.

"You see, I told you," said Zoe. "How can it be?"

"It's impossible," said Mr. Edwards. "Turtles don't grow that much in ten years."

"Well, she has." Zoe traced the letters on her painted shell. "My name isn't growing, though. It just looks smaller because her shell is bigger."

Next morning a turtle as big as a saucer crawled out of the pond. Zoe nearly dropped the tomato she had brought her. That can't be Violet, she thought. But there was the Z-O-E spelled out in violets across the shell. Rather timidly, she put the tomato down before the turtle, who gobbled it in six bites.

She walked slowly back to the house, thinking about the problem. But when she went up to her room, she forgot all about it. In a corner of the top floor of the mouse-house were five thumbnail-sized babies.

"Come on over and bring your order book," she told Ruthie on the phone.

"Oh, no!" wailed Ruthie.

"But we've been waiting for this all summer! Don't you want to talk to all the boys? It's your big chance!"

"Oh, Zoe, you should see me! I just got my braces on!"

But she came over, cutting through the woods. Watching from the window of her room, Zoe saw her stop abruptly by the pond, then get down on her knees to peer at something on a rock. Zoe ran downstairs and outside to meet her.

"Mr. Edwards," Ruthie was saying as Zoe arrived at the pond, "you better watch that turtle. She's so big she'll eat all *six* fish."

Settling himself into the chaise longue with the morning paper, Mr. Edwards answered, "I'm just hoping she gets big enough to eat the duck." Then, putting his hand at the side of his mouth as if he were telling her a deep secret, he whispered loudly, "Every night I come out to the pond and feed her a cake labeled EAT ME!"

"Don't be ridiculous," said Ruthie candidly. "You're much too lazy to do that."

Zoe laughed and then said, "Maybe that's the answer, though. Maybe somebody *is* switching turtles on us every night."

"But who?" asked Mr. Edwards.

"Easy," said Ruthie, after a minute. "Mr. Zuccini. He's the only person who could get turtles — and he painted the shell! He must be doing it."

"Wrong," Mr. Edwards pointed out. "Mr. Zuccini is in Italy."

"I forgot about that," Ruthie admitted. "I can't think very well without my bubble gum."

"Well, we need some thinking done. Come on in the house. I've got gum," said Zoe.

Ruthie sighed sadly. "No good. I can't chew with my braces on. Do you realize I can't have another piece of bubble gum for *two years?*"

"That's awful! But the braces look very nice," said Zoe politely. "I noticed them right away."

"Do you really think so?" asked Ruthie, showing her teeth in a silvery grimace. "You don't think the boys will hate me?"

"Of course not," said Mr. Edwards. "They'll be just as glad to see you coming as they always were."

Ruthie looked at him suspiciously and frowned. "There's something wrong with that statement," she said, "if I could just think well enough to figure it out."

Violet continued to grow. When she got so big that Zoe couldn't pick her up, something had to be done. And then, as suddenly as she had begun to grow, the turtle began to shrink.

"This is unbelievable," Zoe said. "She's two inches smaller than she was yesterday morning." She showed Ruthie the tape measure.

"I can't stand it," Ruthie declared. "She's going to shrink back to her normal size, and we'll never know who did it! I can't stand it!"

"I've asked everybody in the neighborhood if they've seen anything suspicious at night," said Zoe, "but nobody has."

"There's just one way. You're going to have to camp out in the woods and catch whoever it is. Tonight."

"Will you come, too?"

"Sure. I've got to find out who's doing it!"

But when Zoe asked her mother and father for permission, her mother said, "Absolutely not! If somebody's roaming around our back yard in the middle of the night, you're not to be there."

Zoe called Ruthie to tell her the bad news.

"If it were my turtle, I'd do it anyway," said Ruthie. "Nobody's going to hurt you. Wait a minute, Zoe." She talked to someone while Zoe waited, listening to the muffled words. Then she said, "Zoe? My mom says no, too. We'll have to find another way."

Zoe hung up the phone slowly, thinking about what Ruthie had said.

Everyone seemed to want to go to bed early that night, fortunately. Bob was always tired, and Marcia went upstairs shortly after he did. Zoe's mother put out all the lights except a lamp in the hall and went upstairs before the television show Zoe was sitting impatiently through was over.

Zoe stayed downstairs until she heard her father's typewriter stop. After he had gone up, she turned off the hall light and climbed the stairs noisily. She brushed her teeth, humming loudly at the same time, and called good-night to her mother and father's room.

"Quiet," said her father. "Your mother's asleep."

Zoe got into bed without taking off her shorts and blouse and waited, wide-eyed, for an hour. Then she got up and crept very slowly through the hall, down the stairs, and into the kitchen. The key turned in the kitchen door soundlessly, and Zoe tiptoed barefoot onto the porch. She heard the guinea pig rustle softly in his cage. The cricket chirped regularly.

The back yard was not quite dark, but as Zoe opened the screen door carefully to prevent its normal squeak, the moon went behind a cloud and Zoe suddenly couldn't see a thing.

The idea of going all the way to the woods was simply too terrifying. But where could she go? Behind the garage? Who knew what could be lurking there! The doghouse? The very place — she would have some company there.

The yard was damp with dew as Zoe ran lightly through the grass. She bent down and shoved Pudd'nhead's rump aside as gently as she could, and crawled into the doghouse with him. In his corner, Hans rufflled his wings and quacked softly, questioningly. The dog sighed and moved to make room for her. Zoe lay on her stomach, her feet in the air and her arms supporting her chin, and looked out into the yard.

She felt very safe. Even if someone appeared, he couldn't possibly get her in the doghouse. And she had a perfect view of the yard. To her left was the pond, and to her right was the house. The woods behind the pond showed only as a black shadow against the sky, as did the shrubs across the yard. The only thing she could hear was the song of the cicadas. Yawning, Zoe made a pillow of one arm. Her mind drifted from the problem at hand to the opening of school the next week . . .

She woke with a start. She had no idea how long she had slept, or what had awakened her. Pudd'nhead shifted slightly in his sleep and snored softly. Then suddenly she heard another noise, a rustling, as if someone — or something, she thought, shivering — were sitting down in the grass and rubbing against the doghouse.

At the same time the rustling stopped and Zoe began to wonder if she had imagined it, she saw, moving jerkily through the woods, some distance from the pond, a tiny circle of light. It had to be a flashlight.

There he is, she thought. *But who is sitting by the doghouse?*

Straining her eyes to watch the light in the woods, she was distracted by a movement in the middle of the lawn, almost directly in front of the doghouse. In the pale moonlight Zoe made out the figure of a man.

Suddenly she heard the crunch of heels on concrete in the driveway. And then, directly across the yard, the shrubs began to move, although there was no wind at all.

Zoe heard someone cough from that direction. The back door creaked familiarly.

Zoe was confused. She hadn't counted on all this. In the woods the circle of light moved closer to the pond. And then, amazingly, there were *two* circles! A second light moved slowly behind the first one.

Zoe was sure whoever was moving in the grass by the doghouse, a foot from her head, could hear her heart beating. The man in the middle of the yard had disappeared toward the forsythia bushes on the opposite side of the yard. She couldn't see anyone near the porch, but the door *had* creaked, and she could still hear the footsteps in the driveway.

The lights moved steadily toward the pond.

When the moon went behind a cloud, Zoe crawled out of the doghouse as fast as she could. When she was sure she was clear of the porch roof, she stood up and ran as fast as she could toward the house.

Someone tackled her around the knees and she went down, kicking and screaming.

She beat with her fists whoever held her tightly. But at the same time she fought, she heard voices from all sides of the yard.

"I got him! I got him!"

"Ow! Let go! You're killing me!"

"Here he is! Help, somebody!"

"Get off me, you big ox!"

Zoe screamed, "Daddy, help me!"

From the direction of the woods, the gong began to sound madly. Zoe heard a loud splash. Whoever was holding her let go.

"Zoe, is that *you?*" Tooty Thomas asked.

"Well, of course it's me! Who else would be in the dog-house!"

The gong stopped. There were shouts of recognition and puzzlement from all over the yard.

"Bob?"

"Marcia?"

"Ruthie?"

"What's going on here?" The whole yard was suddenly so bright Zoe had to squint. Mrs. Edwards had turned on the lights on the garage as she called from the porch.

"Zoe!"

"Bob!"

"Marcia!"

"Tooty!"

"Ruthie!"

Zoe sat up, blinking, and looked around her. The back yard was littered with bodies. Sprawling on the ground beside her, Tooty blinked back at her.

In the driveway, Bob lay flat on his back. Marcia sat on his stomach. Pudd'nhead and Hans stood side by side in the doorway of the doghouse, looking at Zoe.

Far back in the yard by the pond the chaise longue had collapsed again. Sticking out of the wreckage were Ruthie's head and shoulders. She was holding the gong in one hand and the clapper in the other and staring at the pond. Everyone in the yard was staring at the pond, squinting as they looked.

Dripping and spluttering, muttering outraged threats, Mr. Edwards heaved himself out over the rock ledge.

And beside him, head and feet safely inside her shell, sat Violet. She was miraculously restored to her normal size.

LIBRA

September 23 – October 22

1

"IF THE FIRST WEEK is any sample of the rest of the year,"
groaned Zoe, shifting her heavy load of books to her left
arm, "I may drop out."

"Me, too," Ruthie agreed. "Wait a minute. I can't
stand these shoes another minute."

Zoe sat down on the curb, put her books down beside
her, and took off her shoes and socks, too. She wriggled
her bare, sweating toes. "Boy, that feels good!"

As they picked up their books again, Ruthie said, "You
know, my parents are always threatening to send my
brother away to military school. But I never thought I'd
be going to one!"

"I know. Isn't the Colonel awful? I just don't like men teachers! And blowing that whistle to change from math to science to English is just too much."

"It's the calisthenics I hate," said Ruthie. "All I want after lunch is a nap, and he has us doing push-ups! You're lucky, though. You got out of it."

"Lucky!" Zoe stopped before they turned slowly into Ruthie's yard and stared at her. "You call it lucky to have to do fifty multiplication problems every day? I'd rather do fifty push-ups!"

"He really let you have it because you can't multiply, didn't he?" said Ruthie. "Mrs. Hannum would never have done that."

Zoe nodded glumly. "Mrs. Hannum would never give us homework on the weekend, either. You coming over?"

"I think I'll stay home today," said Ruthie. "If I can get this done today, I'll have two days of freedom."

"O.K.," said Zoe. "I have to practice, anyway, and feed the animals."

"*Practice?* Did you let them talk you into piano lessons *again?*"

"Well — not exactly. I just told them I'd do it."

"But I thought you *hated* piano!"

"I *do*," said Zoe. "But it's not so much trouble anymore. And anyway, it pleases my father."

"Well, it's your funeral," said Ruthie. "Call me tonight."

Zoe cut through Ruthie's yard and the woods to her own yard, and stopped long enough to say hello to Hans and cool her feet in the pond. As she walked slowly toward the house, she heard voices from the back porch and saw Roger there. Not wanting to have to speak to him, she changed her direction so she could go around the side of the house, away from the porch and the driveway, and enter the front door.

But as she reached the corner of the house, she heard a loud thump followed by a peculiar sharp, crunching noise. She looked toward the porch. Roger was leaning over to pick up a book from the concrete floor. His back was to Zoe, and she couldn't see the smaller object he picked up, but whatever it was, he put it back on the floor and pushed it under the glider carefully with his foot. Then he sat down on the glider and opened his book. Zoe moved out of his view, but waited for a minute, puzzled.

She heard Marcia call from the kitchen, "What happened?"

"Just dropped the chemistry book," Roger called back.

Marcia's voice sounded closer now. Zoe risked a look and saw her sister coming out of the kitchen with two glasses of lemonade, which she put on the table in front of the glider.

"Well, let's get this over with," Zoe heard Marcia say. "Pudd'nhead, you'll have to move. Come on, off the glider."

Zoe could see Roger dusting his hands together after he helped Marcia shove the dog off the glider, none too gently. Pudd'nhead walked to the screen door and waited while Marcia held it open for him.

"Why does your sister keep that old mutt around, anyway?" Zoe heard Roger ask. "He's worthless. Should have been put to sleep long ago."

Zoe wanted to go right up on the porch and tell him what she thought of him, but she only gripped her books tightly to her chest and waited.

Marcia said slowly, "We are *all* fond of the dog, Roger.

He's a member of the family. You don't throw away a member of the family just because he's old, do you?"

"You get rid of that smelly old beast and I'll get you a nice poodle, how about that? A pedigreed one."

Marcia laughed a little again, but she only said, "Let's skip it, shall we? We've got chemistry to do."

Zoe hurried around the house, meaning to get her practicing and her homework done in time for her piano lesson before dinner. With Roger on the back porch, the animals would have to wait for their dinner.

She was on her way out the front door, carrying her music, when she saw Mr. Zuccini's truck pull into the driveway. As she ran down the steps, he opened the double doors of the truck and pulled toward him an enormous cage, so big that he hadn't wrapped it entirely, as he usually did. Around the midsection, however, was a wide strip of red and black paper, which prevented Zoe from seeing anything inside except a branch of green leaves.

"Hi, Zoe! Good to see you again!"

"You, too, Mr. Zuccini. Did you have a good time? What in the world is in there? It looks like a tree!"

Mr. Zuccini could hardly see where he was going because of the big cage. As Zoe held the front door open for him, he said, "Run, ask your mother to come!"

Zoe brought her from the kitchen, wiping her hands on her apron.

"Mr. Zuccini, how nice to see you!" she said, looking for him behind the cage he still held. "Did you have a good time?"

"Wonderful time!" he replied. "May we put this pet in flower room?"

"Pet? It looks more like a plant! Wait, let me move some

of these pots." She cleared a place in the center of the semicircular turret area at the front corner of the living room and Mr. Zuccini put the cage down carefully.

When he had stripped off the paper, Zoe could see only a tall branch, planted in a large pot of soil. "Where is it?" she asked Mr. Zuccini.

"There. See. On the leaf."

Zoe looked where he pointed and finally saw a fat, woolly caterpillar, looking like a black and white accordion as it dined on a leaf.

"Will it make a butterfly?" she asked.

Mr. Zuccini nodded. "Any day now, caterpillar will attach itself to branch, shed skin, and metamorphose. In two weeks, Madama Butterfly!"

"I've never heard of a pet butterfly," said Mrs. Edwards, busily arranging the pots of ivy around the cage. "Doesn't it look nice here?"

Mr. Zuccini stood back to admire the effect. The cage looked perfectly natural in its setting of vines and greenery. "Magnificent! Like on stage! And Madama Butterfly good performance, too!"

"How long can I keep her when she comes out of the chrysalis?" asked Zoe.

"Only a day or two. Then let her go with others on long migration. You know what kind of butterfly the caterpillar make, Zoe?"

"If she migrates, it must be a monarch."

"Good! Last of season, too, this one is. But maybe — who knows? — she come back next summer and live in back yard."

Mrs. Edwards looked at her watch. "You'd better hurry, Zoe. You're already late."

Mr. Zuccini saw the yellow music books in her arms. "You go for lesson. Come! I drive you."

"Oh, that's not necessary," said Mrs. Edwards. "It's only around the block. Zoe always walks." She stopped as she saw his disappointed face. "However, if you really want to — "

"Ah! Come, Zoe!"

Zoe returned from her lesson to find the whole house in an uproar. Marcia was on her hands and knees in the hall closet, throwing boots, sweaters, mittens, and scarves into the hall. Mrs. Edwards came out of the study carrying an empty box and three coffee cups. From behind her came Mr. Edwards' voice.

"I've got to find them!" he roared. "I have Important Work to do!"

"Your father has lost his glasses," Zoe's mother told her. "You search upstairs. There'll be no peace until we find them."

Zoe put her music on the chair by the door and took the stairs two at a time. Looking down over the banister, she saw Marcia straighten up, holding a bent metal utensil.

Mrs. Edwards, with a little cry, ran to take the object from Marcia. "The asparagus tongs!" she said. "They've been gone since Christmas."

Zoe looked in the bathroom medicine closet where the glasses had been found the last time. Not there. She checked under her parents' bed and in the cushion of the bedroom chair. Not there.

And as she sat on the rug in her parents' room, thinking of logical places, she remembered something that had happened in the afternoon.

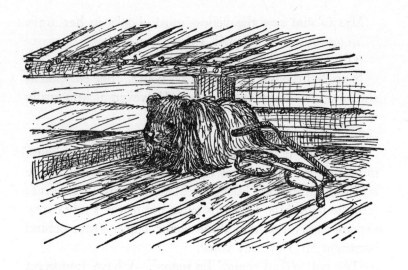

There had been a thump. That was the chemistry book. And there was also another sound. A crunching, as when glass is stepped on.

The glasses were there, in the corner under the glider. So was the guinea pig, but Zoe forgot her when she saw the condition of the glasses. One lens was completely shattered, and fell to pieces as Zoe picked up the frame. The other lens was cracked across the middle.

There was nothing to do, of course, but take the glasses to her father.

"Ye gods! Where were they?"

"Under the glider."

Marcia and her mother came into the study to see them. "But who broke them?" asked her mother, looking at Zoe. "Those weren't just dropped, they were crushed. Zoe, did you —"

"I didn't break them," said Zoe. "If I had, I would have told you."

"Marcia, you surely didn't — "

"Of course not! I would have brought them right to you, Daddy."

"Well, Bob couldn't have," said Mr. Edwards. He looked from one daughter to the other. "We'll just consider it an accident. Perhaps some day the guilty person will have the courage to confess what he did."

"There's no crime in breaking something," added Mrs. Edwards, her eyebrows up and her voice calm. "The fault is in not confessing to a wrong."

Neither Zoe nor Marcia had anything to say. Marcia went directly upstairs and Zoe went to feed the animals.

Crawling under the glider to retrieve the guinea pig, Zoe thought that if she had heard the crunching sound, Marcia surely must have. Why didn't she say anything? It wasn't Marcia's fault. Roger had smashed the glasses with his chemistry book.

There is no crime in breaking something, her mother had said. The fault is in not confessing.

Maybe Marcia would tell her father what had happened. Maybe she honestly hadn't connected the noise with the glasses.

Only one thing was certain. Zoe knew she wasn't going to tell on Roger, and he certainly wasn't going to admit what he had done.

2

ZOE SAT cross-legged in the middle of Bob's bed and sorted socks. "Is college hard?" she asked her brother.

He looked up from the small trunk on the floor where he was packing sweaters. "Harder than high school. But I'll be taking courses I like, so I won't mind."

"I'll bet you'll make a great architect," Zoe told him. "Does this sock go? It's got a hole."

"Throw it over there, in the box. That's right. As for being so great, we'd better wait a few years to decide." He took the pile of socks and began to stuff them into the duffle bag lying by the door. "I've got several years to go yet."

"Well, look at all the things you've already built," Zoe said. "And you're very neat. You're a fast worker, too. It took Marcia three weeks to pack for the summer. You're going for a whole year, and you're through in one evening!"

She sat and watched him silently for a few minutes as he opened the bottom drawer of his chest. Then she said shyly, "Bob? I'll miss you."

He threw a shirt at her. "I'll miss you too, little friend. There are a lot of things I'll miss. Including the big performance. How's the butterfly coming along?"

"Five more days. The chrysalis has been there for nine." Zoe counted on her fingers. "Tuesday! Oh, no! Madame Butterfly's going to come out on Tuesday when I'm in school!"

"Maybe the teacher will let you stay home to watch."

"Are you kidding? Mr. Oldfield wouldn't let me stay home to watch the house burn down! He's as bad about schedules as Mother."

"Does he still run the class like a military academy?"

"Worse! Now we have to jog everywhere, even to assembly. Everybody laughs at us and calls us Oldfield's Army!"

Bob looked up from the pile of shirts he was sorting. "Well, that's Dad's gong. You'd better jog down there quick."

Zoe slid off the bed. "Be right back. Don't pack the records until I get here."

When she reached the back yard, her father was gathering his papers and folders to bring in for the night. He pointed toward the woods and said, "Your turtle keeps heading that way. Didn't you say you wanted to watch where she goes when she gets ready to hibernate?"

"Yes — but it's getting dark, and I'm helping Bob pack."

"Well, you'd better bring her in for the night, because she's not going to be here in the morning if you leave her free. Put her in the terrarium. The Minotaur's never home, anyway."

But since Violet had never been in the house, Zoe couldn't resist taking her upstairs, just to see what she would do. It took a while to coax the turtle out of her shell, but once out, she seemed to enjoy exploring.

By the time the duffle bag was filled and Zoe had jogged on the trunk while Bob struggled to lock it, it was bedtime. Before she went to sleep, Zoe remembered that Violet was still in Bob's room. Oh, well, she thought sleepily, she'll be all right for the night.

But in the morning, in the rush to say good-bye to Bob before she left for school, Zoe forgot Violet again.

After school Zoe went straight upstairs to get her. But Violet simply wasn't in the bedroom. Not in any corner, not in the closet, not in a drawer.

Violet had vanished.

"If that turtle is hibernating somewhere in the house, we won't find her until spring," said Mrs. Edwards. "Search, Zoe. She must be upstairs!"

She had worked her way methodically through the hall, her own bedroom, the bathroom, and was beginning to hunt in Marcia's room when her mother shouted upstairs, "Zoe! Pick up the phone. It's Bob!"

"Hi, Zoe," he said, after she hurried to the extension. "Listen, Violet's O.K. Don't worry about her."

"What do you mean? Where is she? I've looked everywhere and — "

"She's here. With me. We packed her!"

"*Packed* her! You mean she crawled into a suitcase?"

"Into the duffle bag, fortunately for her, because she got air that way. And also, the rest of my luggage went air freight."

"Oh, Bob, what'll we do?"

Bob laughed. "Don't worry about her. The first time any of the guys here in the dormitory come that way, I'll send her. Or I'll keep her until I come Thanksgiving, if you'd rather."

"Oh, send her if you can! She wants to hibernate."

"All right. I'll let you know when she's coming."

"And, Bob? Try to give her a tomato now and then."

"Don't worry about a thing. She's the best-cared-for turtle in the dorm!"

Violet's trip to the university saved Zoe one chore a day, that of going out to the pond with the morning tomato, and Zoe was so busy in September that she was almost grateful for the rest. Sometimes, after a long day

at school and homework, chores, practice, and feeding
the animals after school, she wished she could hibernate,
like Violet, for the winter. And the chrysalis, glowing
green and waxy in the big cage in the turret all weekend,
kept her in such suspense that she could hardly keep her
mind on her regular work, much less the pages and pages
of extra math that the Colonel assigned to her.

The cricket died on Sunday morning.

Zoe found him in his cage, legs in the air, antennae limp,
when she missed hearing his song with her breakfast
tea. The cage had been brought in lately from the porch,
since the evenings were very cool now. Zoe carried it up
to her room without telling anyone at the breakfast table
what was wrong. She had a little cry all by herself in her
room.

"Is something wrong?" her mother asked when she came
downstairs. Zoe wondered for the hundredth time how
she always knew.

"Charlie Cricket died," she managed.

"Oh." It was a long, drawn-out "oh." Her mother put
down the dishtowel. "I'm so sorry, Zoe. We'll miss him."

Zoe nodded and began to dry the silverware. "I knew
it would happen," she said. "Mr. Zuccini said I must take
good care of him, because he was twice as old as most
crickets live to be."

"Yes. You took good care of him."

They worked for a little while in silence. Finally her
mother wiped the sink and said, "Let's go check the
chrysalis. You lost one pet, Zoe, but you're going to have
another one soon."

As they reached the dining-room door, they heard a

crash upstairs and then something bumping down each step of the stairs. Before they arrived at the bottom of the steps, Marcia was already downstairs, picking up a record album. Her arms were loaded with books, records, a stuffed elephant, a rolled up poster, and a large silver picture frame. Without noticing Zoe and her mother, Marcia went straight out the door, kicking open the screen with her foot, and down the steps.

Zoe and Mrs. Edwards watched her dump the things she carried through the open window of Roger's Mustang. She bent over to say something into the open window, and then turned and ran back toward the house. Mrs. Edwards pulled Zoe into the living room before Marcia reached the porch.

Hesitating at the foot of the stairs for a moment, Marcia seemed to change her mind. She walked quickly into the study and closed the door behind her.

She was there a long time, as Zoe knew from keeping an eye on the closed door. Then she came out and went into the breakfast room, where Mrs. Edwards was making posters for her kindergartners. She closed that door, too.

But, although Zoe waited, Marcia didn't come to her.

On Tuesday morning Zoe went straight to the turret when she came downstairs. She took one look and then yelled, "Everybody come quick! She's coming out!"

Mrs. Edwards, already dressed for school, hurried in at the same time Marcia rushed down the stairs.

"Look, look!" yelled Zoe, pointing to the cage.

"Shhh! No use to scream. Your father's still asleep."

The shimmering, top-shaped green chrysalis, which had hung by a few strands of white, thread-like material from the milkweed branch for exactly fourteen days, had a tear at the bottom. Kneeling by the cage, Zoe showed her mother and Marcia the black abdomen of the butterfly that was emerging.

"Can't I *please* stay home and watch it?" she pleaded for the tenth time.

Mrs. Edwards shook her head. "Zoe, we've been all through this. What will people think if teachers' children stay home for no reason? You just have to go."

"For *no* reason! This is a good reason."

"You know what I mean," said her mother.

"Let her stay, Mother," said Marcia. "My biology teacher says you may see this once in a lifetime."

Mrs. Edwards sighed. "Well — come home for lunch. All right? It takes several hours, you know. Probably you can check on it then, and after school you can watch the finale."

That was the best Zoe could do. She ate her toast be-

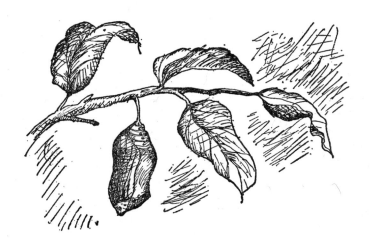

fore the cage, and then called Ruthie to come over before school.

Ruthie squealed when she saw Madame Butterfly protruding from the chrysalis.

"Shhh!" said Mrs. Edwards, on her way out to her car. "Zoe, get dressed. You'll be late. And don't wake your father. He worked very late last night and he may sleep all morning."

Marcia took a last look as she went out the door. "Once in a lifetime," she said. "Maybe I'll come home for lunch, too."

After Zoe had dressed and hurried downstairs again, Ruthie said, "Zoe, why don't you play hooky? Who's to know?"

"Daddy, for one," said Zoe, gesturing toward the stairs with her thumb. "And Mother always finds out things."

"Oh, do it. You can run if your father comes down. I'll bet he wouldn't care, anyway."

"But — I'd have to take a note tomorrow."

"So forge it. No, wait, I'll tell the teacher something happened and that you'll be there late. *Very* late. Then he won't ask for a note, even if you don't get there until two o'clock."

"But — oh, I don't know what to do!"

"Remember what Marcia said," Ruthie reminded her. "Once in a lifetime."

Zoe chewed on her braid and watched the chrysalis, which was now jerking gently as Madame Butterfly fought her way into the world.

"All right," she decided, and threw her braid over her shoulder. "I'll do it. Now, what are you going to tell the Colonel?"

"I don't know yet," Ruthie admitted. "I'm a little slow these days, without my bubble gum, you know. But I'll think of something."

After Ruthie had gone, Zoe made herself a cup of cinnamon tea and tiptoed back through the hall with it. She made herself comfortable on the floor where she could see the living-room door.

Madame Butterfly's performance was very slow. By nine-thirty, Zoe began to worry. At this rate, she would have to leave for school before it was over. What if the Colonel sent the attendance officer? What if her mother called to check on her? What if her father caught her? What if — ?

She froze, with the teacup halfway to her mouth, when she heard the siren. She was almost afraid to look.

When she did, she could hardly believe her eyes.

Down the block, led by a slowly moving police car with its siren screaming and its red light flashing, came Zoe's class, jogging double-time, with the Colonel running beside them, blowing his whistle and counting cadence.

"Right face!" shouted the Colonel, and blew an ear-splitting blast as the sixth grade turned up the walk and jogged right up the steps to the porch. "Class, HALT!"

Zoe opened the door to twenty-four red and grinning faces.

"Are we in time?" asked Mr. Oldfield. He was hardly puffing at all.

"Of course," said Zoe. "Come right in." As Ruthie jogged by her through the door, she whispered, "What did you *tell* him?"

"Easy," said Ruthie. "The truth. Hardly had to think at all."

The class just had time to seat themselves in a semi-circle around the cage when Zoe heard the sound of a loud, heavy motor outside.

"Mother," she said as she opened the door for the twenty-six kindergartners, "what are you doing here? This is *not* on your schedule."

"Nonsense," said her mother. "One must be flexible. Anyway, I reserved the school bus ten days ago. Help me get these children seated before they wreck the house."

They put each five-year-old between two ten-year-olds for safekeeping. Zoe had just rescued the guinea pig, who had apparently spent the night in the turret nibbling ivy, from a small freckled boy when she heard more noise outside.

Without even going to the window first, she opened the front door. Five cars, brakes squalling and horns blowing, pulled up behind the police car and the school bus. The patrolman waved directions to Marcia's entire biology class.

On stage in the turret, the performance of Madame Butterfly continued. The action seemed to speed up a little now, as if the principal actress had only been awaiting her audience before showing all her art. The huge swollen abdomen pushed its way out of the broken chrysalis, and soon the limp and flimsy wings began to emerge. The chrysalis was completely transparent now.

"Why is the body so big and the wings so little?" asked Elmer. "That's not the way a monarch is supposed to look."

"Zoe, can you explain?" asked Colonel Oldfield. "Jog up here, please, by the cage."

Feeling completely ridiculous, Zoe did as he directed.

"The fluid from the body gets pumped into the wings gradually," she began to explain, "and they get larger as the body gets — "

Sixty-five heads turned toward the door to see what Zoe was staring at with such a horrified look on her face.

"Ye gods!" said her father as he fled back up the stairs in his polka-dotted pajamas.

3

Dear Zoe,

There has been a little trouble getting Violet home. You remember I said I would send her with someone from the dorm whenever he was traveling that way. Last Friday one of the guys was called home suddenly, and offered to take her, so I packed her up in a shoebox with a big tomato. The only thing is, my friend had to change planes in Chicago, and he left her on the plane. When he got home, he remembered her, and of course he called the airlines to trace her. The plane went from Chicago to Kansas City and that's where Violet is now. The airline said they will send her directly to you.

Sorry about the mess. My friend said to tell you he was sorry, too, but he's not used to flying with turtles. Don't worry about it. The airlines are very good about these things, and you'll be hearing from them very soon.

Thanks for your letters. Yes, I'll bring you a pennant when I come home at Thanksgiving. Say hello to the Colonel for me.

Love from your brother,
Bob

Zoe waited impatiently for a week, but there was no call from the airline. "Can't we call them?" she finally asked her mother. "I could *walk* here from Kansas City in a week."

"All right. Bring me the phone book."

Zoe brought it and sat at the kitchen table chewing the end of her braid while the call was made. Mrs. Edwards' eyebrows kept going up and up as she talked.

"Well?" Zoe asked, when her mother hung up.

"Well, the man said Violet seems to have disappeared into thin air."

"That's *not* funny! How could she disappear? How many turtles can there be flying to Kansas City in shoeboxes?"

"They searched the plane thoroughly, he assured me. Violet simply wasn't on it." Mrs. Edwards put on her gardening gloves and picked up the trowel from the kitchen counter. "They will continue to search, the man said. She'll turn up."

"I'll never see her again, I just know it!" said Zoe.

"Wait and see, now. The airlines are very good about these things. Come and help me take up the begonias."

The October sunshine was warm on Zoe's back as she knelt with her mother by the flower bed along the back porch, but the breeze was chilly. The lawn furniture had been put away for the winter and the grass was long and filled with autumn insect sounds. Hans floated lazily on the pond, basking in the warmth. Scarlet leaves floated down from the maple to the water.

Zoe held the clay pots for her mother to transplant the begonias so they could be taken into the turret for the winter. "Can we take in some marigolds?" she asked, as she watched the guinea pig nibbling his favorite food behind the row of begonias.

"They wouldn't last, I'm afraid," answered Mrs. Edwards. "But we must try the parsley inside this year. He'll love that."

They dug and potted in silence for a few minutes. Zoe's mind was on her turtle, and it was a shock to her to hear her mother say, "What are we going to do about Hans?"

"What do you mean?" asked Zoe slowly. She knew very well what her mother meant, however.

"It's going to be winter soon, Zoe. The pond will freeze, you know. Don't you think Hans would be better off at the campus pond?"

Zoe had walked on the willow-shaded paths around the campus pond often with her father, and sat on the benches that lined the walks and watched the flock of ducks that lived there. There were a few mallards, but mostly the ducks were the domestic variety, like Hans, often left there in the spring after the novelty of owning an Easter duck had worn off. The pond was spanned by an arched stone bridge, near which was a stone building, which housed the college's nature museum. The foundation of the museum was built at the very edge of the water. There was an opening in the stone where the flock of ducks could swim into shelter in cold weather, and where they roosted at night and were fed by the caretaker of the museum. Zoe herself had often fed the ducks popcorn bought from the pushcart vendor who patrolled the paths around the pond.

But send Hans there?

"He'll be happier there," her mother went on, "than cooped up in the garage all winter alone. And your father —"

"It's Daddy who really wants to get rid of him, isn't it?" asked Zoe. "He even wants to *eat* him for Thanksgiving!"

"Now, Zoe, you know your father was just teasing you."

"He wasn't!" Zoe threw down the empty pot she was holding and got up. "He hates Hans! He always has! And Hans never did *anything* to bother him! It's not fair."

Mrs. Edwards said calmly, "Be reasonable, Zoe. And let go your braid; your hands are dirty. Your father has been very good to you about the animals, in spite of all the fuss he puts up just to maintain his image. After all, he has let Pudd'nhead come in the house now that the weather is so cold at night. And this guinea pig has the run of the whole downstairs. Now you can't ask for more than that!"

Zoe had to admit that her father was tolerant of her pets, but she still knew he hated the duck.

"Think about it," said her mother. "And it should be done soon."

When Ruthie came for the latest batch of mice in the afternoon, Zoe told her what yas going to happen to Hans.

"Sounds good to me," said Ruthie practically as she packed baby mice in her delivery box. "He can find a girl friend there."

"I suppose," said Zoe unenthusiastically. "Wait, that's a parent, not a baby."

Ruthie put the mouse back in its house and tried another one. "You'll miss him, of course," she said, "but you have all the other pets."

"Not really," said Zoe. "Charlie Cricket died. And

Yin and Yang are really Daddy's. And Madame Butterfly flew away. And Violet's in Kansas City."

"Kansas City? How did she get to Kansas City?"

Zoe explained, and then said, "So I'm left with the Minotaur and Pudd'nhead and the Seven Dwarfs and the guinea pig. Oh, I forgot the guinea pig! He's still in the marigold bed!" She put the lid down on the mouse house and hurried out of the room. "Is that enough mice? There should be more in a couple of weeks."

"This is plenty," said Ruthie. "I'm having trouble selling all of them lately. The boys run when they see me coming."

"You should get together with Marcia. She says that's what's happening to her," said Zoe as they ran down the stairs.

"Isn't she dating anybody? What about Hershel?"

"He hasn't asked her. I think she turned him down so often that he won't ask her ever again."

"We'll have to work on that," said Ruthie. "Can I leave the mice here?"

"Not on the kitchen table. Bring them out with you. Now where *is* that guinea pig?"

On Sunday Zoe and her mother took Hans to the pond. Zoe had filled her sweater pockets with oatmeal and coaxed the duck into the guinea pig's cage. They left the car by the stone bridge and walked down the slope to the water's edge.

The willows around the pond were losing their leaves, but the other trees in the parklike area blazed red and orange. People strolled on the paths around the water or sat on the benches in the warm autumn sunlight. Across the pond children threw popcorn to the flock of ducks.

Zoe lifted Hans from the cage and held tight to him while she watched the flock across the pond chase popcorn. "Do you think he knows what they are?" she asked her mother. "He's never seen another duck."

"He knows." Her mother knelt by her, holding out something to Zoe. "Put this around his neck."

It was a little silver chain with a dangling disc on which were engraved Hans' name and birthdate. "From Mr. Zuccini," her mother explained. "You'll always be able to find him when you come to visit."

Zoe fastened the chain around Hans's neck, held him a little longer, and then kissed the top of his head.

Then she let him go.

Hans waddled to the water, then back to Zoe. He quacked at her, holding his head to one side as if he were asking a question.

"Go on, Hans," said Zoe. *"Go on!"*

The duck waddled back to the water and waded in. Zoe stood up and pulled her braid over her shoulder as Hans swam in small circles, then glided straight across the pond toward the flock.

"I hope he likes them," said Zoe. "I hope they like him."

"He'll be king of the pond in no time."

A few ducks on the fringe of the flock swam toward Hans, who stopped in mid-pond, waiting uncertainly. The ducks swam around Hans and then back toward the flock. Hans followed. In a minute, he was lost among the flock, like one small sailboat in a fleet.

Zoe and her mother walked around the pond and Zoe threw her oatmeal to the ducks. Hans, his silver necklace standing out in the crowd of anonymous ducks, caught his share and swam to the edge of the pond. Zoe rubbed

his slick, feathery back once more before she and her mother walked slowly and silently back to the car.

On the stone bridge over the pond, where Zoe could see the stone building with the opening for the ducks, her mother stopped the car.

"One more look?"

Zoe nodded and got out to lean over the high side of the bridge. The ducks, having exhausted the supply of popcorn, glided as one unit toward the center of the pond where the bridge was. As Zoe watched, they swam under the bridge. She ran across the roadway to watch them reappear on the other side after they passed beneath her.

She stared straight down into the water, rippling and glistening in the sunshine, at her own reflection. As the ducks floated lazily under the arched bridge, Zoe saw, glittering in the sun, a little silver circlet on the neck of a duck in the center of the flock.

She watched until it disappeared into the stone shelter.

SCORPIO

October 23 – November 21

1

Hᴏᴡ ᴀʙᴏᴜᴛ Tom Sawyer and Becky Thatcher in the cave?"

"Eccck!" said Ruthie.

"Well, we have to think of *something*," said Zoe. "The party is next week, and we have to make costumes."

"I want something different," insisted Ruthie. "Everybody's going to think of Tom Sawyer."

"I think it's a dumb idea, anyway," said Zoe, "making everyone act out their Halloween disguises."

"I think that'll be fun," Ruthie disagreed. "But I want to look nice with all those boys watching the skits. Hey, there's Mr. Zuccini's truck in your driveway."

Zoe broke into a run. "I hope he brought what I think he did."

"You know what this month's pet is?" asked Ruthie, as she followed Zoe up the front steps.

"Maybe. That empty cage in the turret — "

Mr. Zuccini's black cloak was draped over the chair by the front door, which Zoe stood holding open for Ruthie.

A black bird flew out of the living room, swooped around the hall, and flapped through the dining-room door. Thundering behind the bird came Mr. Zuccini and Mr. Edwards, waving his wife's best linen tablecloth.

"Close the door!" he shouted as he ran past her and into the dining room.

Zoe followed them. The bird had fluttered to rest on the chandelier, where he sat and squawked at the two men running around and around the dining-room table. Mr. Edwards first waved his tablecloth like a bullfighter's cape, and then flung it at the bird.

There was a tinkle and a crash, and the bird flew over Zoe's head and into the hall. Mr. Zuccini and Mr. Edwards rushed to the doorway and stood there puffing, waiting to see where it would land next.

After swooping around the hall again and again, the bird lit on the newel post of the stairway.

Ruthie, still standing by the doorway, said quietly, for Ruthie, "Stay right there." She picked up Mr. Zuccini's cloak from the chair by the door, being careful to make no sudden movements, and inched across the floor to the stairs. Then, with no fuss at all, she dropped the garment over the bird.

"Easy," she said, dusting her hands and displaying all her braces.

Mr. Zuccini gathered cape and bird into his arms and carried the bundle to the abandoned cage in the turret, where he managed to transfer the prisoner.

"How — ?" began Zoe.

"Don't even ask," said her father, and dropped limply on the sofa.

Mr. Zuccini wiped his face with a big red handkerchief and pointed to the cardboard box on the floor in front of the cage. "We had a little trouble getting him in," he said sheepishly.

"What is it?" asked Ruthie, standing with her nose two inches from the bird's yellow beak. "A crow?"

The bird did look like a crow, Zoe could see as she examined it, except for the white circle around his neck. And he seemed smaller, more fragile than a crow.

"Myna bird," Mr. Zuccini told them. "From South Pacific."

"Get me out of here," said the bird.

Ruthie jumped so far she landed in a pot of begonias.

Zoe was delighted. "He talks!" she said. "Daddy, that bird can talk! Did you hear?"

"Great," said her father, rather unenthusiastically.

The bird hopped to the bottom of the cage, back to his perch, over to the side, back again to his perch, squawking and laughing with a raucous, gurgling sound that went up and down a whole octave.

Ruthie sidled up to the cage again. "What else can he say?" she asked Mr. Zuccini.

"Hello," said the bird.

"Ye gods!" said Mr. Edwards.

"That's all he say so far," Mr. Zuccini told him, "but he learn fast."

"How fast?" asked Ruthie.

"Depends on how hard word is, and how many times he hears it."

"Could he learn to say 'Nevermore' in a week?"

"Why, Ruthie?" asked Zoe.

"Because we're going to the Halloween party as Edgar Allan Poe and Lenore," said Ruthie, "and *this* is the raven."

"Get me out of here," said the bird.

"Bird," said Mr. Edwards from the sofa, "if these two have in mind what I think they do, you'll wish you never came in here."

The girls got right to work on their costumes. Zoe found an old charcoal gray jacket of Bob's and cut a tail-coat from it easily enough. Hershel was consulted about what the well-dressed nineteenth-century poet would wear, and came up with a beret under which Zoe could hide her long braid, and, best of all, a flowing artist's tie. With a romantic mustache and a few wrinkles, she thought she would make a passable Poe.

Ruthie arrived one afternoon carrying a decrepit set of gauzelike mauve curtains and asked for help in designing her shroud. Mrs. Edwards complained a little that costume construction wasn't on her schedule, but, fired by the challenge, put Ruthie on a chair and experimented.

"Hold still!" she told Ruthie-Lenore. "You're too lively for a ghost."

Ruthie stopped squirming on the kitchen chair and let Mrs. Edwards drape the curtains into a proper costume for the lost Lenore. "I'm too excited to stand still," she said. "We're going to be so neat-o!"

Zoe put a paper napkin to mark "The Raven" and closed her book. She looked critically at Ruthie's flowing shroud and said, "I don't see why I can't be Lenore. My hair's longer."

"You can't," Ruthie pointed out. "I can't even pronounce all the words in the poem. You'll have to read."

"Turn around slowly, Ruthie," said Mrs. Edwards through the pins in her mouth. "*Slowly!* And tell me again exactly what you're going to do."

Ruthie explained as she inched around on the chair while Mrs. Edwards cut and pinned a ragged hem. "Zoe's going to be dressed like a poet, you see, and sit at a little table reading 'The Raven.' Tooty's dad has fixed up a corner of their basement like a stage, and it'll be completely dark except for a light for Zoe to read by."

"Daddy said we could use the high-intensity lamp," Zoe told her.

"Good. There'll just be a dim glow from it, except on the book. Then, we're going to put Edgar — the bird, not the poet — in my brother's canary cage, which he doesn't need since the canary flew away — "

"I'm not a bit surprised," said Mrs. Edwards mildly. "Stop turning and stand still now."

" — and put the cage up high beside Zoe's table, like on a stepladder or something. When Zoe reads 'The Raven' and the bird comes in, Tooty's going to shine a flashlight on the bird, who is supposed to say, of course, 'Nevermore,' except he hasn't learned it yet."

"Not for lack of trying," said Zoe. "I've yelled 'Nevermore' so much I'm sick of it!"

"So Tooty's going to say it for him?" asked Mrs. Edwards.

"He didn't want to," said Zoe, "but I told him I'd do his math homework for a week."

"He's getting the worst end of that deal," said Ruthie.

"Oh, I don't know," said Zoe. "I'm getting pretty good at it. Hey, I just thought of something. Let's put Tooty under the table with the flashlight. If we cover the side the audience sees with a long tablecloth, he'll have a perfect hiding place."

"But, Ruthie, where do you come in?" asked Mrs. Edwards. "I don't remember Lenore actually being in the poem. The poet just sits and *thinks* about her."

"I'm his imagination," Ruthie said. "The ghost of Lenore. When Zoe reads the name Lenore, I'll just kind of float by, like this."

She climbed down from the chair, holding her shroud carefully until she had both feet on the floor. She spread her arms like a ballet dancer and wafted across the kitchen with her chin in the air. She wafted, in fact, straight into the side of the refrigerator.

"Well, you get the idea," she said, rubbing her elbow.

"I do indeed," said Mrs. Edwards, her eyebrows up. "But do take off your sneakers before you start, Ruthie. And don't smile. Who ever heard of a ghost with braces?"

Ruthie arrived early enough on Halloween night to watch Mrs. Edwards apply Zoe's mustache and wrinkles with Marcia's eyebrow pencil. Her own make-up was fairly spectacular.

"Ye gods!" said Mr. Edwards, as he came into the living room to put Edgar into the canary cage for them. "You look as if you just climbed out of the flour bin."

Ruthie's face and arms were dead white. Under her

eyes were pale blue shadows. Her braces shone brighter
than ever. She had to hold her arms out stiffly so the flour
wouldn't come off.

Edgar took one look at her and said, "Milkman!"

"Dumb bird," said Ruthie, giving the cage a floury
slap. "How did he learn that, anyway?"

"He probably sees the milkman go through the driveway every day," Mrs. Edwards guessed. "He wears
a white uniform, and he always announces himself."

"I think he's pretty smart," said Zoe. "But I hope he
doesn't answer 'Milkman' when I ask him if there's balm
in Gilead."

The doorbell rang as she was getting into her coat and
adjusting the tails.

"I'll get it," said Ruthie. "I need to practice floating."
She slid across the living room and fell over the footstool
in a little floury cloud.

"Ye gods!" said Mr. Edwards, helping her up. "No wonder Lenore died young. She was definitely accident-
prone."

"Don't dust me off," said Ruthie with some dignity, and
continued floating to the front door, considerably sur-
prising the Western Union messenger who stood outside.

"You want bubble gum or taffy?" Ruthie asked him.

"Telegram for Miss Zoe Edwards," said the messenger.

Ruthie took it, surprised. "Really? I thought that was
your trick-or-treat costume."

"She has to sign," said the messenger.

Puzzled, Zoe signed his book and opened the yellow
envelope. "It's about Violet! Listen, everybody! 'Turtle
located. Flying home from San Francisco. Explanation
follows.' Hurrah!"

"How *could* she have gotten to San Francisco?" wondered Mrs. Edwards.

"Well, we can't worry about that now," said Ruthie. "Let's go, Zoe. We're first, you know. How do we look, Mr. Edwards?"

Zoe's father inspected them critically as they stood side by side. "Positively Gothic," he said, "except I never heard of Edgar Allan Poe wearing bell-bottom blue jeans."

Zoe looked down and giggled. "It won't matter. They won't show in the dark." She picked up the poetry book and handed Ruthie the cage containing Edgar. "Just one more thing," she said, and took the small statue from the lid of the piano.

"You're taking *that* to the party?" asked Mrs. Edwards.

"This is the pallid bust of Pallas," Zoe explained.

"Is that what that is?" asked Ruthie. "I always wondered. Who's Pallas, anyway?"

"Pallas Athene, goddess of wisdom," said Mr. Edwards.

"But this is Beethoven," Zoe said, holding up the statue. "Remember, in 'The Raven' the bird sits on the pallid bust of Pallas over the door?"

Ruthie inspected the statue. "Well, he doesn't look too wise, but he sure looks mean enough."

Mr. Edwards threw back his head and laughed.

"You sound just like your bird," Ruthie told him. "Come *on*, Zoe!"

Tooty's house was completely dark. They knocked at the basement door at the far side of the house and waited. From inside they could hear earsplitting screams, moans, and the clanking of chains.

"That's Tooty's dad," Ruthie said. "He loves Halloween as much as the Fourth of July."

"Well, I hope this bird behaves better than the dog did then," said Zoe.

A white-sheeted ghost let them in and led them down a dark hallway to the Thomases' basement family room, where they waited outside the door until Tooty came out. He wore a skeleton costume.

"Where you guys been?" the skeleton asked. "Everybody's ready to start."

"We didn't want them to see our costumes," said Zoe. "Can you get everybody to sit down and turn off the lights before we go behind the curtain?"

Tooty managed, with the help of his mother and father, to get the attention of twenty costumed sixth-graders. When they were seated on the floor in front of the corner where Mr. Thomas had stretched a blanket to hide the stage area, he turned off the lights.

Immediately twenty screams went up, and in the confusion Zoe and Ruthie slipped behind the blanket and turned on the flashlight to prepare the stage.

The table, covered with a long round cloth, was in place near the curtain. The stepladder was propped against the wall, with room for Ruthie to move across the stage behind the table and in front of the ladder. Zoe put the canary cage on the top rung and the statue of Beethoven on the step below. Tooty sat down crosslegged under the table and took the flashlight. When he aimed the beam at Edgar, the bird ruffled his wings and cocked his head to the side, but kept his mouth shut. Zoe hoped it would stay shut.

When Ruthie was in place behind the chair at the corner of the stage where she would hide until time for her entrance, Zoe sat down at the table, turned on the tiny lamp, and focused the light on the book.

"Ready," she said to Mr. Thomas, and the blanket was pulled to the side of the stage opposite Ruthie's hiding place.

The audience quieted immediately. Zoe knew that all they could see was a sad poet, reading by a tiny light in his study. The rest of the stage was so dark that the stepladder was hardly visible. She began.

"Once upon a midnight dreary, while I pondered, weak and weary,
Over many a quaint and curious volume of forgotten lore, —
While I nodded, nearly napping, suddenly there came a tapping,
As of some one gently rapping, rapping at my chamber door."

"It's 'The Raven,'" somebody in the audience announced.

"Shhhhh!"

"Quiet!"

"Shut up!"

Zoe went on:

"Eagerly I wished the morrow; — vainly I had sought to borrow
From my books surcease of sorrow — sorrow for the lost Lenore,
For the rare and radiant maiden whom the angels name Lenore . . ."

Perfectly on cue, Ruthie glided across the stage silently, her ghostly face eerie in the faint light, her trailing cur-

tains exactly shroudlike. The audience rustled. Ruthie
vanished into the blanket folds.

Two stanzas later, when Zoe came to

"But the silence was unbroken, and the stillness gave no token,
And the only word there spoken was the whispered word,
*   'Lenore!' "*

Ruthie glided by again from her hiding place behind
the blanket folds and disappeared behind the chair,
which was invisible to the audience. The audience
rustled and whispered, but when Zoe began again, there
wasn't a sound.

"Open here I flung the shutter, when, with many a flirt and
*   flutter,*
In there stepped a stately Raven of the saintly days of yore.
Not the least obeisance made he; not a minute stopped or
*   stayed he;*
But, with mien of lord or lady, perched above my chamber
*   door . . .*
Perched, and sat, and nothing more."

Under the table, invisible to the audience, Tooty
beamed the light on Edgar, who fluttered his wings ef-
fectively. The audience applauded.

"Ghastly grim and ancient Raven wandering from the Nightly
*   shore:*
Tell me what thy lordly name is on the Night's Plutonian
*   shore!"*

Tooty turned the flashlight on Edgar and croaked
spookily,

"Nevermore!"

The audience loved it. They whistled and clapped. Enjoying the performance herself, Zoe read with great expression for several more stanzas, through the parts of the poem where the poet tries to figure out why the raven has come to his room, and whether the bird will leave him, as his other friends have done, and finally decides that the bird is sent as a prophet. The audience sat perfectly quiet in the dark basement and listened intently as Zoe read and the bird appeared in a beam of spooky light at the end of each stanza to croak, "Nevermore."

Toward the end of the poem Ruthie had another entrance.

" 'Wretch,' I cried, 'thy God hath lent thee — by these angels he hath sent thee
Respite — respite and nepenthe from thy memories of Lenore!
Quaff, oh quaff this kind nepenthe, and forget this lost Lenore!' "

Quoth Tooty,

"Nevermore!"

And Ruthie glided soundlessly from her hiding place, arms spread, head up, and fell flat over Tooty's outstretched feet. Beethoven teetered precariously and toppled off the stepladder onto Ruthie's prone body.

"Tooty!" hissed Zoe. "Get your feet back under the table!" No one could hear her in the hoots and howls of laughter.

"My legs were going to sleep!" Tooty whispered back.

Zoe waited, seething, while Ruthie picked herself up, replaced Beethoven on the ladder, and limped off-stage to hide behind the curtain.

The audience never did become perfectly quiet again. The spell was broken. When the laughter had subsided somewhat, Zoe went on, but she had to read louder to be heard.

> " *'On this home by Horror haunted — tell me — tell me truly,*
> * I implore:*
> *Is there — is there balm in Gilead? — tell me, I implore!'* "

Zoe could feel the table shaking with Tooty's silent laughter. When he didn't respond to the cue, she gave him a good, swift kick. He managed to gasp,

> *"Nevermore!"*

and then exploded into laughter.

The audience broke up again. Zoe could see people rolling on the floor, holding their sides. She waited patiently. The whole thing didn't seem to matter anymore. When there was relative quiet, she had to almost shout to be heard. The next stanza was interrupted by giggles and cackles.

> " *'Tell this soul with sorrow laden if, within the distant Aidenn,*
> *It shall clasp a sainted maiden whom the angels name Lenore —*
> *Clasp a rare and radiant maiden whom the angels name*
> * Lenore!'* "

Tooty quoted properly and the light shone on Edgar. Zoe couldn't understand the burst of laughter from the audience until she heard Ruthie behind her, struggling with something. Risking a look around, she saw Lenore enveloped in the blanket, trying to fight her way free. Little clouds of flour puffed from the folds. When she finally freed herself and floated by again, Ruthie's ghostly pallor had completely disappeared.

Two more stanzas, thought Zoe. Only two more. She had to shout to be heard.

" *'Get thee back into the tempest and the Night's Plutonian
    shore!*
*Leave no black plume as a token of that lie thy soul hath
    spoken!*
Leave my loneliness unbroken! quit the bust above my door!
*Take thy beak from out my heart, and take thy form from off
    my door!'* "

Before Tooty could collect himself, Edgar cocked his head to one side in the sudden light and said clearly,

"Get me out of here!"

The audience sat in stunned silence for a minute and then screamed with glee. Determined to finish or die trying, Zoe stood up on her chair, bell-bottomed jeans and all, and shouted at the top of her lungs,

*"And his eyes have all the seeming of a demon's that is
    dreaming,*

*And the lamp-light o'er him streaming throws his shadow on
    the floor;*
*And my soul from out that shadow that lies floating on the
    floor*
Shall be lifted —"

When Tooty turned on his flashlight, every boy and
girl in the room suddenly stood up and yelled with him,

"Nevermore!"

2

Maybe he's asleep by Pudd'nhead in the study," said
Ruthie, crawling out from under the dining-room table.
"I don't see why you don't keep him in his cage, or put a
bell around his neck, like a cat."

Pudd'nhead was snoring on the hearth as usual, but
the guinea pig wasn't there. Nor was he in the front hall
closet, where he liked to sleep among the boots if he found
the door ajar.

"Can't you leave her out until we get back?" asked
Ruthie, plopping down on the stairs. "The first good day
for sled riding, and we're spending it hunting for a
guinea pig!"

"Go without me if you want to," said Zoe unenthusiastically. "I have to find her before I can go out."

"Get me out of here," called Edgar from his cage in the
turret.

"Did you look in there?" asked Ruthie.

They found the guinea pig crouched behind a pot, nibbling begonia leaves.

"Thanks, Edgar," said Zoe.

"Milkman," said Edgar.

Zoe picked a few leaves to put in the guinea pig's cage in the breakfast room. Putting fresh water in his bottle, Zoe said, "He really misses being outdoors."

"Can't you let him out on the porch when there's no snow?"

"Oh, no. Guinea pigs are very sensitive to cold. That's one reason he should be in his cage and not running around the drafty house. But he likes to explore so much I just can't bear to keep him cooped up."

They were putting on their coats in the front hall when the doorbell rang.

"Oh, no!" wailed Ruthie. "We're never going to get to the hill. All the boys will be gone!"

A pretty young lady in a blue cape and red boots smiled at Zoe when she answered the door. "Zoe Edwards?" she asked. "I have something that belongs to you. All the way from San Francisco." She held out a shoebox.

"Violet!" said Zoe and Ruthie together.

"Is that its name?" the lady asked. "The boy who kidnaped her called her George." She peered into the box at the turtle, who pulled in head, arms, and legs, when the lid was removed.

"*Kidnaped* her!" said Zoe.

The stewardess opened her purse. "He's sorry he did it, though," she said as she handed Zoe a letter. "His mother made him write and apologize."

Zoe read the letter while Ruthie asked the stewardess

if it were true that airline stewardesses got married as quickly as the ads say.

"He says he carried her all the way from Kansas City to San Francisco under his coat," she told Ruthie. "He had her a month before he told his mother."

"He really didn't mean to steal her," said the stewardess. "He thought she had been abandoned. And he wants you to write and tell him how she's getting along."

"Is he cute?" asked Ruthie.

"Who?" asked the stewardess.

"Never mind," interrupted Zoe. "Thank you very much for returning her, ma'am. I'll be sure and write to the little boy."

After she had gone and Zoe and Ruthie had put Violet in the terrarium with the Minotaur, Ruthie said, "You should tell the little boy about how the turtles were switched last summer. Didn't you ever find out who did it?"

Zoe shook her head.

"One of these days we will," said Ruthie. "Come *on*, Zoe! It's going to be *dark* before we get to the hill, and it'll probably all be gone in the morning."

But there was more snow during the night.

"Two more inches!" said Mrs. Edwards, sipping her tea and looking out the breakfast-room window at the white world. "If this keeps up, Bob won't be able to come home for Thanksgiving."

"He'll get here," said Zoe. "He promised."

"Even Bob can't get a plane off the ground in a blizzard," said Mrs. Edwards as she pushed back her chair. "Ready, Marcia?"

"Ready." Marcia stood up, too. "Can we give you a lift, Daddy?"

"I'll get my briefcase," answered her father. "What is this Christmas shopping in a normal month, anyway? I thought it was on the schedule for July."

"We thought of something *somebody* would like," said Marcia, grinning at Zoe mysteriously.

"Zoe, are you sure you don't want to come?" asked Mrs. Edwards.

Zoe shook her head. "Ruthie and I are going sled riding."

"Well, be sure you do the dishes first. And for heaven's sake, find that guinea pig."

Zoe was searching for the lost pet when Ruthie called. "Hurry up," Ruthie said, "the snow's going to melt before we get there."

"I lost the guinea pig again."

"Did you look in the turret?"

"He's not there today."

"Well, if you're not here in five minutes, I'm going on."

Zoe searched frantically in the study and the dining room. No guinea pig. Finally she thought, Nobody will be here all day. I'll be back before they will. They'll never know.

Hurrying so Ruthie wouldn't leave without her, she put on coat, boots, and mittens, wrapped her muffler around her neck, and ran across the back yard to take the short cut to Ruthie's house.

She didn't come home until after four o'clock. Cold,

tired, and wet, she took off her frozen boots on the front porch and stepped into the front hall. With a shock, she realized that the floor was almost as cold as the front porch.

Something's open, she thought, slamming the door. She ran through the hall, following the draft from the dining room to the kitchen.

The back door was standing wide open. Cold air poured in. She shut the door quickly and leaned against it, glad no one was at home to see what she had done. But the house was freezing.

The thermometer in the front hall said 50 degrees. Cautiously Zoe turned up the dial of the thermostat and then, still in her coat and wet slacks, went through the house closing doors so the rooms could warm more quickly. The breakfast room, on the opposite side of the kitchen from the draft that had blown through the back door toward the dining room, was not too cold. She hesitated before shutting the door and then saw the guinea pig's empty cage.

Frantically she searched all the places she had searched before. After making a complete circle of the house, she came back to the kitchen and sat down at the table. Her hands were shaking, she saw, from cold or fright.

She looked at the back door. She got up, not wanting to open it.

Oh please, she thought, *don't let him be out there.*

The guinea pig was huddled in the corner where the glider had sat in the summer. The furry little body shivered as Zoe picked it up.

She went into the breakfast room and huddled on the

sofa, putting the guinea pig under her coat and her sweater, next to her own warm body. She was still there when the front door slammed.

"Good heavens, it's cold in here!" Zoe heard her mother say as she came through the house. "Zoe? Where are you, Zoe? Oh, Zoe, Zoe, *whatever* is wrong?"

She slept late from sheer exhaustion and woke with a start.

"He seems all right," said her mother in the kitchen. "I couldn't get the vet. Just a recording because it's Sunday."

Zoe bent over the cage, which they had filled with pieces of an old woolen blanket, and stroked the soft hair.

"I wouldn't pick him up, Zoe. Let him rest. Animals should be let alone when they're sick."

"I know that," said Zoe, wishing the guinea pig would nuzzle her hand, or stand with her front paws against the bars and oink. "Did he eat?"

"No. He drank though, out of the dropper. He seemed very thirsty. Get your clothes on, Zoe. You'll be sick yourself if you run around in pajamas and no shoes."

Zoe dressed and ate her toast, sitting on the floor by the cage. The guinea pig lay quietly in her blanket, not moving, all morning.

At lunchtime Zoe tried without success to swallow the chicken soup. When she went back to the cage, the guinea pig was breathing rapidly. His reddish brown midsection moved up and down as he lay on his side.

"I'm going to try the vet again," said Mrs. Edwards. Zoe pulled her braid over her shoulder and chewed on the end as her mother dialed the number. With relief, she heard her mother begin to talk, explaining that the guinea pig had been out in freezing weather for an unknown period of time, maybe an hour, maybe more.

"He's calling a prescription to the drugstore," Mrs. Edwards said, replacing the receiver. "He says it's pneumonia, and to keep him warm and give him liquids, which is what we're doing."

Mr. Edwards went for the medicine. He didn't complain about having to go out. When they mixed the dark liquid with water and put it in the dropper, the guinea pig drank it thirstily and then slept.

Late in the afternoon Marcia said, "Zoe, go and rest for a while. I'll sit with him."

Zoe got up slowly, stiff from staying in one position for so long. She went upstairs and lay down for a few minutes, then got up and cleaned her room, even getting out the vacuum cleaner. Then she did her extra arithmetic homework, all of it. She went downstairs again, hesitating at the bottom step, and then went into the living room. She practiced for thirty minutes.

When she came back into the kitchen, Marcia got up without a word and Zoe sat down again by the cage.

At dinner time her father brought her dinner to her. When her mother picked up the untouched plate, she said nothing to Zoe, but made a chocolate milk shake in the blender. Zoe drank it all.

"Bring the cage back into the breakfast room and put it by the radiator," Mrs. Edwards said when the dishes were cleared away. "You can lie on the sofa and watch television."

"Is it time for more medicine?" asked Zoe.

"Yes. I'll get the dropper."

The guinea pig lay quietly under the blanket all evening, eyes bright, breathing labored. Zoe could hear him gasp — short, quick, wheezing sounds. When she stroked his side, she could feel the heat.

At eleven her mother said, "Go to bed, Zoe. You have to go to school tomorrow. I'll stay up and give her the medicine at midnight."

"Can't I stay? I couldn't sleep anyway."

Her mother sighed, but she said, "All right. Cover up with the afghan."

They watched the news and part of an old movie called *Home for the Holidays*, which reminded Mrs. Edwards of Bob's Thanksgiving visit.

At twelve the guinea pig was dosed again. He drank only a little. His breathing seemed to get in the way of his drinking.

"Can I take him upstairs?" asked Zoe. "By my bed?"

When her mother nodded without looking at her, Zoe knew the guinea pig was going to die.

They carried the cage upstairs and put it by Zoe's bed, where she could touch the guinea pig. Mrs. Edwards stayed in Zoe's room while Zoe put on her pajamas and brushed her teeth.

Zoe closed her eyes when her mother kissed her good night so the tears wouldn't show. When she was sure her mother was in bed, she sat up and turned on the lamp by the bed.

She wrapped the guinea pig in the old blanket and held him close, propped up on a pillow. The house was very quiet. Across the room, the Seven Dwarfs scuttered about their house, wondering why a light was on at such a strange time. Through the windows Zoe could see wet snowflakes hit against the glass. She saw that it was one o'clock.

The guinea pig moved feebly in his blanket and nuzzled her braid. She could hear the wheezing sound again.

Please, please, don't let him die, she prayed silently. She closed her eyes to keep a tear back.

She woke suddenly. Her face was wet, and the clock told her she had only dozed for a minute or so. She shifted the guinea pig slightly in her arms. The wheezing was worse. She stroked the long white hair and remembered the first time she had sat and held her pet like this, on the porch with Hershel's music coming out the French doors to her. She remembered the guinea pig's explorations in the marigold bed, the oinking for breakfast, the naps by Pudd'nhead in the study.

"We never even gave you a name," she said aloud, and kissed the hairy little nose.

She held the guinea pig close to her chin and felt the little animal nuzzle her neck feebly. He wriggled a little, and then the wheezing and the wriggling stopped, and he was completely still.

SAGITTARIUS

●

November 22 – December 22

1

Bob came home for Thanksgiving on a cold and sparkling day and received a hero's welcome. Mrs. Edwards made a tremendous effort with dinner, which she even served in the dining room, and got a grudging compliment from her husband.

"Very nice," he said, as they sat down at the table gleaming with the best china and silver. "Why can't we do this every night?"

Mrs. Edwards groaned.

"This is the first time I can remember just the family eating in here since Zoe came home from the hospital when she was four days old," said Bob.

"Did I eat with you?" asked Zoe.

"No, you were upstairs in your crib," said her father, "squalling through the whole horrible meal, as I remember. Have a yam."

While he struggled through his second piece of mince pie, Bob asked Marcia about her social life.

"Pretty depressing these days," she said. Zoe hoped she would mention Roger, but she said no more.

"I don't believe you don't get plenty of offers," said Bob.

"She gets them," said Mr. Edwards. "Phone rings day and night."

Marcia poured herself more coffee. "Not very interesting ones."

"Well, if you're not busy tonight," said Bob, "would you like to go to the new coffee house? I hear the music is pretty good."

"I'd love it!" said Marcia.

"Can I go?" asked Zoe.

"Sorry, chicken. You're too young." Bob looked at her carefully and grinned. "However, in about three years, the boys are going to be taking you places."

"What!" cried Mr. Edwards, pulling down his glasses to look at his younger daughter. "Zoe? She's just a baby!"

"I am not," said Zoe firmly. "I'm going to be in junior high school in nine months and one week."

"Ye gods!" said her father. "I never thought of that." Then, sipping his coffee, he said to Bob, "I might come along with you if you don't mind. I'd like to hear Hershel read some of his poetry."

"That's not fair," said Zoe. "If I'm too young, you're too old."

But, surprisingly to Zoe, her father wasn't too old for the coffee house.

"You should have seen him, Mother," said Marcia at breakfast. "He was the life of the party."

"He knew everyone there," said Bob. "There must have been twenty people at our table all night."

"All those lovely college men," said Marcia, chewing her eggs glumly. "And all with dates."

"My entire Elizabethan lit class was there, reading blank verse to guitar music," Mr. Edwards explained to his wife. "It was horrible."

"Did Hershel read poetry?" asked Zoe.

"He was there, but he didn't read," said Bob. "The muse probably deserted him when he saw Marcia. Anyway, he's taken up psychiatry."

"He spent the entire evening analyzing everybody except *me*," said Marcia, helping herself to more bacon.

"You sound disappointed," said Zoe slyly, but Marcia went on.

"I never realized before that Hershel had so many friends," she said. "Hershel must have some hidden qualities I haven't considered."

Zoe caught her father's eye over the toast platter and he winked at her. Zoe laughed.

"What's so funny, you two?" asked Marcia.

"Some of us," said Zoe, "have known about Hershel's hidden qualities for a long time."

Marcia played with her eggs instead of eating. "Well, I'd certainly like to be analyzed," she said.

"Work on it, Marcia," said Bob. "Zoe, are we going to the pond?"

"I'll get the oatmeal," said Zoe, jumping up.

Except for a few hardy ducks near the bridge, the pond and the campus were deserted. The bare willows drooped over the still surface of the pond, bright and clear in the winter sunlight. Bob and Zoe were the only people on the path. Even the pushcart vendor was gone.

"Let's go up and look over the bridge," said Bob, and they climbed the slope to the roadway over the stone arch. Zoe leaned over to look at the ducks' home under the museum.

"Throw some oatmeal and they'll come out," said Bob.

Quacking greedily, the ducks paddled out of the opening in the stone wall as the oatmeal made tiny ripples on the water. Zoe squinted in the sunlight and then pointed. "There's Hans! See the silver necklace?"

"He looks fat and healthy," said Bob, trying to aim his oatmeal at him. "Hello, Hans!"

The duck, who was busy racing his friends for the food, looked up briefly and then turned to the oatmeal.

"He's forgotten us," said Zoe sadly.

"Maybe not. In the spring, when it's warmer, you can stand at the edge and he'll eat out of your hand like he always did."

They watched the flock for a while. When Zoe got tired of tiptoeing to see over the high, wide bridge side, Bob lifted her up so she could sit. They watched in silence for a minute. Then Bob said, "I'm sorry about the guinea pig, Zoe."

Zoe looked at the ducks and said nothing.

"I guess you miss him a lot."

Zoe looked at the ducks, not at Bob, and nodded. "He was the best pet of all. We — we buried him in the marigold bed."

"You don't want another one? Mom said Mr. Zuccini offered one for this month's pet and you refused."

"I'm not going to take any more pets," Zoe said slowly, pulling her braid over her shoulder, "this month or next. It's all over."

"Anyone could forget to close a door tightly, Zoe."

She shook her head. "I was careless and selfish. I was in a hurry and I didn't take care of him and he died. I don't deserve any more pets!"

Bob took the end of the braid from her and held it between his gloved hands. "I think you're being a little hard on yourself. You've always taken good care of the pets. You know that."

"Except once."

"Yes. Only once."

"And look what happened." Zoe grabbed her braid back and hesitated a moment. "But there's — another reason, too."

"For not wanting another pet? Go on."

Zoe reached into the oatmeal box for a handful and threw it to the ducks before she continued. "Remember when Mr. Zuccini came to dinner with the monkey, and we talked Daddy into letting me have the animals?"

"Yes, of course."

"And Mother said the pets might be a good idea because they would teach me responsibility. And you agreed. You told Daddy I should take the pets on approval. Remember?"

Bob nodded. "You made some promises. You told us you would keep your room clean and learn the multiplication tables — "

" — and practice every day and take care of the pets. And I haven't done any of those things the way I should have! I did just what I had to do, and no more, and I complained all the time." Zoe tried to keep her voice calm. "I told you. I don't *deserve* another pet!"

Bob stared into the water for a while and then said quietly, "I see."

Zoe chewed her braid and kicked her heels against the bridge side where she sat. The wintry sun went behind a cloud. Bob turned up his coat collar as the wind began. Below them, the ducks quacked and looked up expectantly.

Bob threw a handful of oatmeal and watched the ducks race across the pond for it as the wind scattered the flakes. "I thought your room was clean when I got home yesterday," he said.

"I cleaned it for you. But I've been keeping it clean since — "

"And you practiced a long time last night. Sounded pretty good, too."

"I've been practicing better all month."

"And didn't I see a good arithmetic paper tacked up on the bulletin board?"

Zoe nodded. "But that's really because of the Colonel. All that awful extra work — but now I'm doing it because I know I have to."

"You finally figured that out, did you?"

"Yes — you see, I found out that if you can multiply, you don't have a bit of trouble with long division! Did you know that?"

"Did I — but, Zoe, how in the world did you do long division before you could multiply?"

She shrugged her shoulders and answered sheepishly, "I didn't, unless I had time to do a lot of adding. Anyway, the Colonel caught me adding on my fingers and really lowered the boom."

"So now you're doing all right?"

"Yes — and you know something else? Doing arithmetic is just like playing the piano. I don't mind it so much now that I've stopped complaining about how to do it. And even Daddy says I sound better."

Bob grinned. "That's high praise!"

Zoe frowned a little and brushed oatmeal crumbs out of her braid. "Of course, he may be just being nice to me because of the guinea pig. Even if he didn't like it."

"Oh, I think he liked it. I think he really likes all the pets, Zoe. He just won't admit it because he's protecting his mean-old-man-of-the-mountain image."

"Maybe," said Zoe doubtfully, looking down at Hans. "But he made the duck leave home."

"That had to be done, Zoe."

She nodded. "I guess so. And you know, Daddy *has* been nice to Pudd'nhead. He lets him sleep in the study in front of the fire — and when we first got the dog, Daddy wouldn't let him in the house! Now he's using Pudd'nhead for a footstool in front of the rocking chair. Did you see?"

"I saw him. Dad told me he was glad to find something 'that monster' was good for."

Zoe laughed. "You want to know a secret? About Daddy?"

"What?"

"Last week I caught him in the turret *talking to Edgar!* He kept looking around to see that nobody was watching, and whispering 'Ye gods.' "

Bob hooted with laughter.

"Don't tell him I know about it. He'd be embarrassed," Zoe said.

"I won't. But he certainly has damaged his image!"

They laughed together and Zoe shook the last of the oatmeal out of the box. She shifted her position on the stone side of the bridge and said, "My bottom's getting cold."

"We'd better go home. Say good-bye to Hans."

As Bob lifted her down from the side of the bridge, Zoe said shyly, "Bob? I'm glad you're home."

"I'm glad to be here," he answered, setting her on her feet. "And Zoe? You think about another pet. I think you're beginning to keep your promises pretty well."

Zoe looked up at him. "I'm changing my image," she said, grinning. "Like Daddy."

Bob laughed and yanked her braid. "Come on — race you to the car!"

2

THE SCHEDULE on the kitchen bulletin board allowed Mrs. Edwards until the fifteenth of December to have her Christmas cards mailed, her dinner cooked and frozen, her gifts wrapped, and her house decorated.

She almost made it.

"Ridiculous!" said Mr. Edwards, leaning against the door of the study and watching his wife hang mistletoe from the chandelier in the hall. Marcia and Zoe were draping the stairway banister with pine boughs.

"The proper expression, Daddy," said Marcia, "is 'Bah, humbug!'"

"A little originality, please," said Mr. Edwards, and stalked back into the study to his Important Work.

"Daddy's a real Scrooge, isn't he?" asked Zoe, tying a red velvet bow around the newel post.

Mrs. Edwards climbed down from the stepladder and inspected the mistletoe. "Of course not," she said. "He enjoys Christmas as much as anybody else. He's just keeping up his image."

"I don't see him saying 'ridiculous' to all the work you have to do for the faculty party," said Marcia. "Is it the Saturday night before Christmas this year? Oh, there's Mr. Zuccini." She had stopped and looked out through the glass in the front door.

The bells on the holly wreath jingled as Zoe opened the door for Mr. Zuccini. He had a red ribbon on his black hat, and holly pinned to his cape collar.

"Merry Christmas, all!" he boomed. "Am I allowed a Christmas kiss under the mistletoe?" He bowed and kissed Mrs. Edwards on the hand, and Zoe on the forehead.

"Don't forget me," said Marcia. "I like that hand bit."

"House beautiful for Christmas!" said Mr. Zuccini, admiring the stairway. "Sure you don't want to sell? I may need nice house soon!"

"Would you consider a second mortgage?" called Mr. Edwards from the study. "The way these women spend money at Christmas, we may need one."

Mr. Zuccini peeped into the living room. "No tree?"

"Not until Thursday," answered Mrs. Edwards. "With Bob gone, it's hard to get it up. Hershel promised to come and do it."

"Would you like to come and help decorate it?" asked Zoe.

"Thursday? Ah, can't come Thursday! Another little party, around — " he gestured toward the front door.

"You mean — ?" Zoe began.

"Yep! Hey, Zoe, out in truck — "

Mr. Edwards interrupted from the study. "Come and have a look at my bettas, Mr. Zuccini. I think they have the ich."

Zoe followed him into the study, where he bent over the aquarium containing the Siamese fighting fish. He stroked his mustache thoughtfully as he studied the fish. Then he said, "Don't have ich," he said. "Fish have neurosis."

"You've been listening to Hershel," said Mr. Edwards.

"Right. Learn all about psychology. Fish are frustrated. Need outlet for hostility."

"You mean *let them fight?*" asked Zoe.

"Right. Been staring at each other through that glass for months. All droopy from trying to get at each other."

"You take out the glass partition," said Mr. Edwards, turning his back and covering his eyes. "I can't bear to watch."

Zoe watched Mr. Zuccini lift the glass partition from the tank and place it, dripping, on the hearth. The fish at first didn't realize that they could now tear each other to bloody shreds at will. But when they accidentally bumped noses, they immediately displayed gorgeous scarlet and indigo fins and tails and began to circle each other strategically.

"Wonderful!" cried Mr. Zuccini as Yin tore a piece from Yang's tail. Mr. Edwards flinched and buried his face in his hands.

"Let him have it, Yang!" shouted Zoe.

Mr. Edwards turned around at this. "Would you two

bloodthirsty barbarians like to place bets? I'll hold the money."

"Come on, Yang!" shouted Zoe as her fish countered by diving for Yin's tail.

"Bravo, Yin!" yelled Mr. Zuccini.

"Watch out, Yang!"

"Good shot, Yin!"

After a few minutes of fierce fighting, the fish swam to opposite corners of the tank, like fighters after the bell. They were sad-looking creatures now, fins and tails tattered and torn. Mr. Zuccini inserted the glass partition in the middle of the tank between them.

"That's all for this time," he said. "They have hearty dinner now."

Zoe surveyed the ruins. "Will they get well?"

"Sure. Be better than ever in little while." He turned to Mr. Edwards, who pulled down his glasses to peer at the fish, pure horror on his face. "You let them have good fight every month or so. Keeps them healthy."

Mr. Edwards looked doubtful, but when he sprinkled some protein food on top of the water, the fish gobbled it greedily.

"See?" said Mr. Zuccini triumphantly. He turned to Zoe, and his expression changed. "Zoe, go out and look in truck. On front seat."

Zoe looked at the floor and said, "Mr. Zuccini, I don't —"

"You go look. Bring inside. You not want it, say so. But look."

She put on her coat slowly, thinking, I won't take it. I won't.

The box on the front seat was a red cardboard carrying case with black zodiac signs decorating the front. Cautiously, Zoe opened the top.

Looking up at her with blue, strangely crossed eyes was a pale, fragile kitten which yawned elaborately, stretched, and began to uncurl.

I won't take it, thought Zoe.

She put her mittened hand into the box, and the kitten immediately attacked. When she jerked her hand away, the kitten came too, clinging tightly to the mitten. Zoe saw that its tail had a funny little crook at the end. She held the kitten against her coat and stroked its back.

I won't take it, she told herself.

Mr. Zuccini had said to bring the kitten inside. When Zoe put it down on the hall rug, everyone oohed and aahed and gathered around it.

"He is King of Siam, Zoe," said Mr. Zuccini. "You like him?"

"He's beautiful!" Marcia exclaimed, trying to rescue her charm bracelet from the kitten's clutches. "But is he Siamese? He's so light."

"Markings change as he gets older," Mr. Zuccini explained. "He is good cat. Maybe win ribbons in shows later. You like him, Zoe?"

Mrs. Edwards knelt by Marcia and tried to protect her stockings from the sharp little claws. "Good heavens, he's active!" she said. "Isn't this rather an expensive pet for Zoe, Mr. Zuccini?"

Mr. Zuccini shrugged his shoulders and grinned. "Question is, does Zoe *want* him?"

Zoe, retying her father's shoelace after the kitten had climbed off his foot, said nothing.

"Vicious little brute, isn't he?" muttered Mr. Edwards as the kitten pounced on a scrap of mistletoe and rolled over and over with it.

Mr. Zuccini's paunch bounced as he laughed. "Very kinglike. Zoe, do you want him?" He looked at her anxiously.

Zoe took a deep breath and stood up. "I want him, Mr. Zuccini. I'll take good care of him."

"Ah!"

The King of Siam saw his own tail, abandoned the mistletoe, and gave chase.

The Christmas tree wasn't trimmed on Thursday, as scheduled, because that was the day the King of Siam climbed the pine tree.

It was Mr. Edwards, opening the front door to get the morning paper, who let him out. The kitten bounced down the steps, tail in the air, looking for worlds to conquer, and chose the pine tree. Before Mr. Edwards could reach him, he was halfway up.

"Helen! Marcia! Zoe! Help!"

Marcia's window above the porch went up and she put out her pink-curlered head. Zoe and her mother appeared at the front door.

"The King of Siam's in the pine tree!" shouted Mr. Edwards, waving both arms and pointing up the trunk.

"That sounds like a limerick," said Marcia. "The King of Siam's — "

"Very funny. Get down here!"

By the time Zoe got her coat on and ran outside, the kitten had found a suitable branch and crawled out a little distance. There he crouched comfortably, swishing his tail and surveying his domain.

Zoe tried vainly to lure him down with kind words and tasty morsels of bacon. The kitten wouldn't move. He was so far up the tree that she got a crick in her neck from watching him.

"You'll have to go to school," Mrs. Edwards said as she came outside with her books. "Your father will be here all morning, I think. He'll let him in the house when he comes down."

"But it's so cold!" said Zoe, shivering in the wind.

"He'll come down when he gets hungry," said Mrs. Edwards.

At lunchtime Zoe called her father. "Is he down?"

"Who?"

"The King of Siam!"

"Oh! No, he's still up there. He'll come down when he gets hungry."

But he wasn't down when Zoe ran home from school. The cold wind through the pine tree carried piteous little meows to Zoe all the way to the corner.

Zoe stood under the tree calling his name. He meowed, but he didn't move.

"Daddy, what are we going to do!" she wailed, as she shut the front door.

"He'll come down when he gets hungry," called her father from the study.

"Will you stop saying that? I had *lunch* and I'm hungry. He hasn't eaten since *last night!*"

Mrs. Edwards's car pulled in the driveway as Zoe went back outside. They both stood under the tree staring up, listening to the kitten cry. The December twilight came early. The wind quickened as the streetlights came on. The kitten huddled close to the tree trunk, meowing.

"Do something, Daddy!" said Marcia, as they came out to join Zoe under the tree before dinner.

"If only Bob were here!" said Zoe.

"Well, he's not, and the kitten can't stay there until Saturday," said Mrs. Edwards. "We'll have to call the fire department. John, you do it."

Grumbling, Mr. Edwards went into the house. When he returned, he sat down on the bottom step and cupped his chin in his hand.

"*Well?*" Marcia asked.

"Haven't you ever read a story about a fireman coming to rescue a kitten, with ladders and everything?" he asked.

"Sure," said Zoe. "Happens all the time."

"Sorry," said her father. "It's a myth."

"Call the S.P.C.A.," said Mrs. Edwards promptly.

Mr. Edwards groaned, but he got up and went in the house. Then he came back and sat down again, chin in hand.

"*Well?*"

He looked at Zoe and frowned. "They say they don't rescue kittens from trees, but if necessary, they'll come and remove the — the carcass."

There was a silence. Zoe sat down on the steps by her father. In the pine tree the wind whistled and the kitten meowed.

"If only Bob were here," repeated Zoe.

Marcia started up the steps two at a time. "They're not going to remove this kitten's carcass," she said grimly as she reached the door. "Give me five minutes."

They waited four. Then, loping along the sidewalk toward them, came Hershel. His black cape was draped over a long aluminum extension ladder.

Everybody stood up and cheered.

Hershel set up the ladder, which Marcia insisted upon holding steady for him. He removed his gloves and handed them to Mrs. Edwards, who folded them tenderly. He handed his cape to Zoe, who held it draped over both arms in front of her.

He shook hands manfully with Mr. Edwards and mounted the ladder.

Up he slowly went, as far as the ladder would take him. Then he stepped to a branch and climbed slowly, cautiously, from limb to limb. Sometimes he had to work all the way around the trunk to progress one foot up the tree. But he kept going.

Below him, Zoe clutched the cape with her braid between her teeth. Mrs. Edwards twisted Hershel's gloves. Marcia stood, still gripping the ladder, although Hershel was several feet above it now.

Mr. Edwards rubbed his aching neck. "I can't stand it any longer," he said, and went to sit on the steps.

After he climbed a few more feet, Hershel began to talk to the King of Siam. Zoe could hear only a few words, the rest carried away by the wind. Suddenly she saw Hershel's arm shoot out and heard the kitten begin to howl ferociously. It was almost too dark now to see, but she could make out a writhing, squirming bundle apparently clinging to Hershel's beard.

"He should have his gloves," Mrs. Edwards said, realizing that she was twisting them in her own hands.

"You're worried about *gloves?*" said Mr. Edwards incredulously. "He should have a parachute."

They watched tensely as Hershel began the long climb back down the tree. The trip was made more difficult by

the furious, frightened kitten, which Hershel tried to hold on to with one hand.

No one said anything. Hershel came slowly down, foot by foot. Zoe forgot the crick in her neck. Mr. Edwards came to stand at the base of the tree again.

Hershel carefully transferred his feet to the ladder, still using the limbs about him for handholds. Then both hands were on the ladder. Zoe let out a long-held breath.

"Now, that wasn't so bad, was it?" asked Mrs. Edwards.

"He's not down yet," muttered Mr. Edwards.

Marcia clutched the ladder more tightly as Hershel's weight made it slide a little on the frozen ground. Then, as his foot came within reach, she let go one side, reached up and patted his ankle, and said, "Hershel, you're wonderful!"

Mr. Edwards said later that it must have been Marcia's praise that made him dizzy, or the touch of her hand on his ankle. Whatever the cause, Hershel's feet slipped off the ladder and he half slid, half fell the rest of the way down, landing at the foot of the ladder with one leg doubled under him peculiarly.

The King of Siam bounded from Hershel's beard to the ground and bounced across the lawn and up the steps, where he stood meowing at the front door, demanding to be let in.

CAPRICORN

●

December 23 – January 20

1

Isn't it beautiful!" said Zoe, squinting to make the colored lights blur and shimmer. "We should take a picture of it."

Sparkling with silver tinsel and icicles, gleaming with red and blue ornaments and lights, the Scotch pine stood in the curve of the piano. The silver star at the top almost reached the ceiling.

"Lovely," agreed Mr. Edwards, and then added, as they all stared at him, "ridiculous, but lovely."

"I wish Hershel could see it," said Marcia.

"How was Hershel this morning?" asked her mother, packing leftover ornaments into a box.

"Oh, he's fine. The cast can come off in six weeks, and he gets to come home for Christmas."

"Poor Hershel!" said Zoe, who thought it unfair that children under twelve weren't allowed in patients' rooms. Everybody except her had gone yesterday to see Hershel, and Marcia had gone back alone this morning.

"Poor Hershel, my eye!" said Marcia. "You should have seen that room this morning. There were so many people there I thought I'd gone to the coffee house by mistake. And he had a tree, and presents, and a record player, and — "

"Did you take him a present?" asked Mrs. Edwards. "After all, he saved the life of the King of Siam."

"Daddy paid for it, but I chose it," said Marcia, and giggled. "I gave him an electric razor."

"Ye gods!" said her father. "You never give up, do you?"

"Actually," said Marcia, "I think I rather like the beard. It suits him now he's taking up the guitar. What are you looking at, Daddy?"

Mr. Edwards had suddenly pulled his glasses down from his forehead and was staring intently at the Christmas tree. "The King of Siam," he announced, "has found another pine tree."

It took half an hour to get the kitten out. He would not be coaxed from his perch on a limb over the piano. Finally Mr. Edwards put on his overcoat and gloves as protection against scratchy branches and claws, reached into the depths of the tree, and pried the King of Siam loose. The kitten, after being dumped rather ungently on the rug, headed for the tree again. Zoe dived for him.

Whenever he could sneak into the living room, the King of Siam climbed the Christmas tree. Try as Mrs. Edwards would to keep the doors to the room closed, the kitten found a way in. A determined dash across the room, or a stealthier route behind the sofa and around the corner to the piano, a mad climb up the trunk, and he sat, a solid, furry little ornament, while the tree shivered and ornaments crashed to the floor.

The tree began to look a little tatty. The tinsel hung vertically in ropes instead of draping gracefully around the tree. Icicles bunched unartistically. The rug below the tree glittered with bits of glass. The star became permanently cock-eyed.

Bob came home from college several days before Christmas and was introduced to the King of Siam who, naturally, was in the tree at the time. "That tree looks as if it's been stored in the garage all summer and brought out to be used again," Bob pronounced.

"What are we going to do with it?" asked Mrs. Edwards frantically. "The faculty party is in two days. I can't bring all those professors and their wives in and let them see this mess!"

Zoe clutched the King of Siam, who struggled to get out of her arms, and said, "It doesn't look so bad in the dark."

"I think she's right, Mom," said Bob, trying to correct the tree's tendency to lean toward the center of the room. "Just keep the room dark except for the tree lights."

"Use candles," suggested Marcia. "Lots of candles. All over the house. No one will ever notice. A little to the right, Bob. That's it."

The Edwardses' annual faculty party was almost a tradition with them after so many years, but it was a terrible strain on Mr. Edwards. All week long he watched anxiously as his wife cleaned the house from top to bottom, ordered food and drink, baked cakes and hors d'oeuvres, and got out the punch bowl and the party plates. He wandered around the house getting underfoot, offering unwanted advice, questioning arrangements, and generally driving his wife wild.

"Are you sure this is enough punch?" he asked, counting the rows of gallon jars chilling on the back porch.

"That is enough punch," said his wife grimly, "for an entire campus riot. Go feed your fish."

He wandered into the dining room and disarranged the centerpiece on the table. "Are you sure we shouldn't get someone to serve?"

"Marcia can do it beautifully," answered Mrs. Edwards tiredly. "She always does. And Bob will do kitchen duty. And Zoe will take the coats at the door. It's all on the schedule, dear. Stop worrying!"

He lighted all the candles and turned off all the lamps to try the effect. In the soft glow, the Christmas tree looked almost normal. "I just hope no one decides to play the piano and turns on the lamp there," he muttered.

"They won't," said Mrs. Edwards. "The piano is locked. Will you *please* go write a letter to the editor or something!"

On the evening of the party, Zoe, splendid in a new red velvet jumper, and with a red ribbon woven into her braid, waited in the front hall for the first guests to arrive. Mr. Edwards came downstairs in his dinner jacket.

"Daddy, you look beautiful," said Zoe.

"So do you," he said, squinting elaborately with his hand to his forehead, "I think. Where are you?"

"Daddy, it's not *that* dark!"

"Is that cat locked up somewhere?" he asked.

"In the study with Pudd'nhead."

"In the *study?* But — "

"Mother locked that door, too. She said it's the only place in the house that looks worse than the Christmas tree."

By eleven o'clock, when Zoe's mother told her to go to bed since surely no one else would be coming, the house was full of people, all laughing, arguing, standing in groups, milling about, drinking and eating. Zoe put on her pajamas and robe and sat for a while in the dark at the top of the stairs, watching people come and go. She wondered why it was that adults never seemed to sit down at parties.

Looking down the stairway at a group of people at the bottom, she admired or criticized all the women's clothes and decided that she liked best a very short, glittery dress worn by a pretty lady who had come with one of the bachelor professors. Her father seemed to like that lady, too, since he spent a lot of time talking to her at the foot of the stairs. Zoe heard him telling the pretty lady something about fish.

She was stretching and yawning and about to go to bed when she saw something downstairs that made her shut her mouth so hard her teeth clicked.

Trotting purposefully through the hall, his tail up like a question mark, came the King of Siam. He brushed by the hem of a long skirt, stepped daintily over a pair of polished black shoes, and disappeared into the living room.

Mr. and Mrs. Edwards were nowhere in sight. Aware of her flannel robe and fuzzy slippers, Zoe slipped down the stairs as quickly as she could, hoping no one would notice her in the dim lighting.

No one seemed to pay the least bit of attention to Zoe as she edged around clusters of people and made her way through the hall and the living room. As she peeped around a large gentleman standing near the sofa, she saw that the Christmas tree, which was shivering slightly, contained in the middle a large, dark blob. Then, as she watched, the tree began to tilt very slowly forward.

Zoe cut around another group of guests to the tree and waded into the prickly branches to grasp the trunk. She righted the tree. When she let go, it began to lean again. Frantically looking over her shoulder for her father or mother, Zoe stood surrounded by branches and held the tree up.

Above her head, the King of Siam settled himself to watch the party. Zoe tried to find a more comfortable position, since it looked as if she might be there for some time, and hoped no one would notice her. The noise and laughter in the darkened room seemed louder, but the guests seemed unaware that anything was wrong. Her arm was getting tired.

A large lady in a long, shiny dress billowed across the room toward the tree. "Why, Zoe, my dear, how you've grown," she gushed.

"Yes, ma'am," said Zoe, trying to look as if she always stood around in Christmas trees at parties.

"How old are you now, dear?" cooed the lady.

"Eleven — twelve in June."

"Eleven and a half exactually?" chanted the lady gaily, waving her punch cup.

I'm being stabbed to death by a Christmas tree and my arm is falling off and she's *quoting* to me, thought Zoe, trying to look around the lady's bulk for her father.

"And where do you go to school, dear?"

Zoe had had as much as she could take. "State

reformatory, ma'am," she said calmly. "They let me come home for Christmas. Good behavior."

"Oh! Oh, well — I — oh!" The lady backed away, stuttering. Zoe pushed a branch off her forehead and gingerly changed her position so she could hold the tree trunk with her other arm.

The next person who noticed Zoe in the tree was the pretty lady in the glittery dress.

She strolled over, smiling, and said, "Do you know you have a cat in your Christmas tree?"

"Yes, ma'am," Zoe gasped.

"Would you like me to hold the tree for a while?"

Zoe looked at her bare arms and shoulders. "No, ma'am. Just, please, get my father quick."

The pretty lady laughed and ran away. She returned almost immediately, laughing still and leading Mr. Edwards through the crowd. Zoe noticed that her father didn't seem to mind being dragged along at all. Quite a few heads turned to watch their progress. A few people followed them to the tree. Zoe wished she had something on besides her old flannel bathrobe.

The pretty lady pointed and said to Mr. Edwards, "You have a cat in your Christmas tree."

"You should have been here the last time," Zoe's father said, taking in the situation. "My daughter's boy friend broke his leg getting him out."

"Daddy," said Zoe faintly, "to quote Edgar, get me out of here."

"Broke a leg getting him out of *that* little tree?" asked the lady doubtfully.

"Stop asking questions and go get Don," Mr. Edwards told her as he reached over Zoe's head through the branches. An ornament landed on her shoulder. "I've got it now, Zoe. You can let go."

Zoe backed out of the prickly tree and rubbed her sore arms. The pretty lady came back again, still laughing, with her bachelor professor in tow. More people came to stand before the tree.

"Anne says you want me to hold your Christmas tree," said the young professor, puzzled.

"Take my place here, will you?" asked Mr. Edwards. "I have to get the King of Siam out."

As Mr. Edwards moved out of the tree, the other man reached around his shoulders and took the trunk in his hand. Mr. Edwards stretched upward toward the kitten. The crowd of onlookers had grown still more.

"There you go, you stupid cat," said Mr. Edwards. He peeled the King of Siam from his perch and was promptly scratched for his pains. He flung the cat to the rug. The polite spectators applauded.

Zoe grabbed him as he headed for the tree again.

"Well, I'll be!" said the young professor. "I thought that tree looked a little — "

"Don't let go! Oh, no!"

"TIMBER!" yelled somebody. The guests scattered.

Mr. Edwards just had time to shove Zoe and the King of Siam out of the way before the tree fell on him.

2

THAT'S GOOD, ZOE. Hurry up, before he falls in."

The flash bulb exploded and the King of Siam leaped

off the edge of the aquarium to Pudd'nhead's back. Zoe clicked out the spent bulb and wound her Christmas camera to the next number.

"That's a really neat present," said Ruthie.

"Isn't it?" said Zoe. "I don't know how they knew I wanted one. I hardly hinted at all." She aimed the camera at the kitten, now washing his face on Pudd'nhead's broad shoulders.

"Let's go see if the food's ready," said Ruthie. "I'm starved."

"Why are we having high tea?" Mr. Edwards was asking his wife as Zoe and Ruthie entered the living room.

Mrs. Edwards put down a tray of teacups. "I really don't know what the occasion is. Mr. Zuccini called this morning and asked if we would be at home, so I asked him and Hershel to tea. Hershel wants to see Bob before he goes back to college, anyway."

"There's the truck," said Bob from the window. "Why, he's brought Mrs. Petrovich!"

"I knew it!" said Ruthie, as she and Zoe ran down the front steps to meet them. "Something's up!"

They all had to help Hershel out of the back of the truck, where he had ridden so he could keep his leg, in plaster to the knee, stretched out. Mrs. Petrovich fluttered about underfoot as they guided him up the steps with his crutches.

In the living room, Marcia put a pillow behind Hershel and Mrs. Edwards lifted his cast to the footstool. "Everybody sit down, please," said Zoe's mother. "Hershel, let me fix your tea for you. Milk or lemon?"

Zoe and Ruthie sat on the floor at Hershel's feet and inspected his cast. Instead of the usual autographs, the plaster was covered with red and black zodiac signs.

"Mr. Zuccini painted your cast for you!" said Zoe, looking for the Gemini sign. She found it on Hershel's heel.

"No, no," said Mr. Zuccini. "Hershel painted it. Very talented boy."

Zoe was puzzled. "But these are the same as the signs on the truck and in the shop," she said slowly. "I always thought *you* painted them, Mr. Zuccini."

"Me? I'm no painter! Truck was white until Hershel came to work for me, remember? And shop."

Zoe thought for a minute. She pulled her braid over her shoulder and munched the curl at the end. A great realization was dawning on her.

At the same time she opened her mouth to speak, Ruthie squealed, "And who — *who* painted Violet?"

Hershel grinned slowly and looked at Mr. Zuccini, who said, "They catch you, Hershel! Took them a while, but they did it!"

"They almost caught me that night in the back yard," Hershel said. "If I hadn't seen Ruthie following me through the woods with a flashlight, it would have been me that Ruthie pushed in the fishpond and not Mr. Edwards."

"But how did you do it?" asked Zoe. "How did you switch those turtles?"

Hershel shrugged his shoulders and grinned again. "I just took a bigger one out of the shop every night and brought it to the pond," he said. "Lured the other one out with a tomato slice."

"But the Zodiac was closed that month," said Zoe. "Mr. Zuccini went to Italy."

Mr. Zuccini began to chuckle, his paunch and his teacup quivering. "Hershel was in shop every morning," he said. "Somebody had to feed the animals, you know."

Ruthie frowned and said, "Why, I never thought of that, Zoe. Was that before or after I got my braces and gave up bubble gum?"

"Awful hard to keep secret," said Mr. Zuccini. "Almost told you many times." Then he smiled broadly and added, "Speaking of secrets, have one to tell you now."

"I knew it," said Ruthie, as Mr. Zuccini heaved himself to his feet and gallantly helped Mrs. Petrovich to rise.

"I have honor to announce," he said, "that Klara consent to become my bride!"

Mrs. Petrovich waved her handkerchief and uttered little cries as congratulations were showered on them. Mr. Zuccini beamed and bowed in all directions.

"A toast!" said Hershel, and raised his teacup. "To Mr. and Mrs. Zuccini: may their circle of animals and friends increase!"

"Hold it!" said Zoe, and aimed her camera.

"Don't put your cups down," said Mrs. Edwards, after they had drunk. "I'd like to propose another toast."

Zoe, Marcia, and Bob looked at each other questioningly as their mother stood up and raised her cup in Mr. Edwards's direction.

"To Professor Edwards's new book," she said, "which will be published this year."

It was Mr. Edwards's turn to beam and bow.

Zoe asked, "Does that mean all the Important Work is finished?"

"No, no," said her father. "I'm just getting a good start.

Now I can finally get to all those letters!" He accepted a fresh cup of tea from Marcia and said, "I have a toast, too. Let's toast the animals."

Marcia said, "I'll begin it. To Charlie Cricket!" She raised her cup.

"To the Minotaur," said Ruthie, and downed her tea.

"To Pudd'nhead and Hans," said Bob.

"To the Seven Dwarfs," shrilled Mrs. Petrovich.

"To Yin and Yang," said Mr. Edwards.

"To Violet," said Mr. Zuccini. "But wait — "

"To Madame Butterfly," Mrs. Edwards interrupted him.

"To the King of Siam!" said Hershel, and everybody laughed.

"Don't forget Edgar!" Mr. Edwards added.

"To the guinea pig," said Zoe quietly, and drank her tea.

"Wait, wait!" said Mr. Zuccini, heaving himself off the sofa again. "Zoe's zodiac not complete yet! No pet in November, remember?" He started for the door.

"Here we go again," said Marcia.

Mr. Edwards put his head down on the arm of his chair.

Zoe rushed to the window. Mr. Edwards came to stand beside her as they watched Mr. Zuccini opening the doors of the Zodiac truck outside.

He pulled toward him a cage, a big one, with a strip of Zodiac paper wrapped around the middle.

As Mr. Zuccini picked up the cage, something dangled from the underside of it, something long, and brown, and curling.

"Ye gods!" said Mr. Edwards.

Zoe ran to open the door for Mr. Zuccini and the last pet of the year. She found she couldn't remember its name. But it was something literary, she knew.